maybe

# maybe

## BRENT RUNYON

ALFRED A. KNOPF
NEW YORK

THIS IS A BORZOI BOOK PUBLISHED BY ALFRED A. KNOPF

"Blister in the Sun"
Written by Gordon Gano
Copyright © 1980, Gorno Music (ASCAP)
Used with permission from Gorno Music (administered by Alan N. Skiena, Esq.)

"I Have a Dream"
Copyright © 1963 Martin Luther King Jr., renewed 1991 Coretta Scott King.
Reprinted by arrangement with the Estate of Martin Luther King Jr.,
c/o Writers House as agent for the proprietor, New York, NY.

www.randomhouse.com/teens

Educators and librarians, for a variety of teaching tools, visit us at
www.randomhouse.com/teachers

*Library of Congress Cataloging-in-Publication Data*
Runyon, Brent.
Maybe / Brent Runyon. — 1st ed.
    p.  cm.
SUMMARY: Sixteen-year-old Brian struggles with life at a new school, his sexual desires, and his unresolved feelings about the loss of his older brother.
ISBN-10: 0-375-83543-1 (trade) — ISBN-10: 0-375-93543-6 (lib. bdg.)
ISBN-13: 978-0-375-83543-8 (trade) — ISBN-13: 978-0-375-93543-5 (lib. bdg.)
[1. Death—Fiction. 2. Brothers—Fiction. 3. Sex—Fiction. 4. Interpersonal relations—Fiction. 5. Schools—Fiction.] I. Title.
PZ7.R888298May 2006
[Fic]—dc22
2005036268

Printed in the United States of America
October 2006
10 9 8 7 6 5 4 3 2 1
First Edition

*For Christina Egloff, who was the architect of great portions of this book, and is the smartest, kindest, most dedicated person I've ever known*

This sucks. We're moving. The truck just left with all our stuff and my mom and dad are waiting for me in the car. We're about to leave. I can't believe this. I can't believe we're moving away from the only place I've lived in my whole life.

I lean into the car and say, "Wait, I think I forgot something."

I go back into the house one last time. It's so weird to be in here with everything empty. The couch used to be right there. There's an impression in the carpet where it used to be—the ghost of a couch.

I walk down the hall to my room. There's nothing left. The posters are off the walls—all that's left are a few pieces of tape and the hole from when I tried to do a flip and put my foot right through the drywall.

My brother's room is right across the hall. The door is closed and I don't want to open it. When we were little we used to barricade ourselves into his room with those cardboard bricks and then bust through like we were the Incredible Hulk. I know it's empty, but I just can't stand to open the door and look in. I don't want to see it empty. I want to remember it full.

There is a sign on his door that he made in Shop class. The word *Maybe* carved into the wood. It's stuck on the door with some heavy-duty adhesive. Mom told me to leave it because she didn't want to ruin the door. Fuck that. I tear it off, and some of the paint with it. I just want to have something.

I run out the front door and slam it behind me one last time. My parents are still waiting in the car. They're sitting in the front seats being totally quiet. My dad is driving, my mom is crying, and I'm sitting in the back by myself.

# ONE

**M**om drives me to my new high school. Classes start in three days, and I'm supposed to meet my new guidance counselor and choose my schedule. Jesus, why do I have to do this? Why can't someone else do this for me?

I'm sure my guidance counselor is going to be some old guy in a terrible suit and a tie that's about six inches too short and just lies on his belly. He's going to have this terrible breath and probably be mixing whiskey in with his coffee.

Mom drops me off out front and says she's going to do some errands. "I'll pick you up in an hour." An hour? Why do I need a whole hour?

I walk through the front doors and stand in the lobby.

The school is totally empty. When a place that is usually

full of people is totally empty, it's really weird. The floors are all waxed and shiny, and it smells like heavy-duty toxic lemon cleaner.

The only place that even has lights on is the main office right in front of me.

The lady behind the desk is old but has jet-black hair and one eye that is looking at the door I just came through. The other eye is looking at me.

She says, "Hello, son. Can I help you?" Her voice is unbelievably high—like a fire-engine siren.

I say, "I'm here to meet my guidance counselor."

The lady is wearing a muumuu—like the thing that people from Hawaii wear, except I don't think she is from Hawaii. She asks my last name and I tell her, and she searches for a while in this really ancient computer and then looks up at me and at the door and smiles.

She says, "You're with Mr. Scott."

"Okay, how do I find him?"

"Follow the drumming."

I walk out of the office and stand in the hall for a second. Was she saying that Mr. Scott was like the band director or something? There isn't any drumming that I can hear.

Wait, now I hear the drumming. It just started. It's not, like, crappy jazz drumming or marching-band drumming, it's straight up rock-and-roll drumming. Real kick-ass—bass-snare-ba-bass-bass-snare—drumming.

I walk down the hall toward the sound. I get so close I feel the bass drum in my chest.

I pull open the doors to the auditorium and stand in the

back and watch the guy play. He has his drum kit set up in the orchestra pit, and he's just going crazy on the drums.

He has long hair and he's wearing some sort of cutoff shirt, and his arms are a total blur.

I move closer to get a better look at how fast his arms are moving from drum to drum, and then he sees me and stops. "Hey," he says. "Sorry, I didn't know anyone was in here."

I say, "You didn't have to stop." I mean, he's a pretty damn good drummer.

"No. No. I'm almost done." He's out of breath. "Do you need me for something?"

"Well, I don't know. I guess you're supposed to be my guidance counselor."

"Whoa. Okay. Cool. Let's do it."

He takes me back to his office and fills out a bunch of forms for me. He signs me up for all my required classes: Latin II, Chemistry, English, Algebra II, and U.S. History. I sign up for an elective called Visual Language, because it sounds cool and I like movies.

He says, "Okay, Brian, you've got one elective left. Third period. And the only classes that are open are Shop and Chorus." He looks at me like the choice is pretty obvious. Take Shop and get your fingers cut off, or take Chorus and learn something about music.

My brother took Shop, so I sign up for Chorus.

# TWO

First day of school. I grab my book bag and go out the garage door and across the street to where they tell me the bus stop is.

I don't know if I have the right book bag. It's black and it only goes over one shoulder, like a bicycle-messenger bag. These are supposed to be what everyone uses these days— that's what the lady at the store said anyway. I hope so.

I stand next to the street sign on a carpet of dead pine needles that crunch under my sneakers. We live on a long dead-end street, and all the houses here are pretty spaced out, so I'm the only one at this particular bus stop, which is fine.

I stand still and look around the neighborhood. This place is so stinking flat. That's what I hate about it most. I mean, I guess it's pretty cool to be so close to the ocean, but I can't stand how flat it is.

Actually, the highest point in fifty miles is a landfill that they turned into a state park and call Mount Trashmore. Seriously, Mount Trashmore.

Finally, the bus comes and stops right in front of me. The bus driver is a lady, and she says something to me that I don't quite hear, because I'm already casing the entire bus looking for a good place to sit.

I used to sit in the back of the bus, at my old school, but I'm not sure if that really extends beyond zip codes. I sit in the first empty seat on the right side and slide over to the window.

There are a few girls, probably freshmen, sitting in the seats near me, and they're giggling and joking with each other. I remember when I was a freshman. That seems like so long ago now, even though it was only two years ago. That's weird. So much has happened since then.

"J.J. told Molly that he wanted to get his dangle in a tangle." They all giggle. I'm not sure what that's supposed to mean, exactly, but it's clearly something sexual.

The only other person sitting in the front of the bus is a girl with snarled dark hair. There's obviously something wrong with her. Most people wouldn't go out of the house with their hair like that, snarled and begging for a brush. And her clothes are Salvation Army—sweatpants that are too small and a multicolored striped shirt that should have been removed from circulation at the end of the Carter Administration.

The bus stops and a few more people get on. Two boys who are rowdy and kind of tough-looking. They must be brothers.

There's also a short girl. She sees some people she knows in the back and jumps up and down, like she can't believe that they're here. She's cute.

The last guy to get on is different than everyone else. He's got long, dirty blond hair—not like the color dirty blond, like blond hair that is dirty—like a surfer, and it's hanging down into his face, and he's wearing a winter jacket even though it's almost seventy degrees. He carries himself like he's afraid somebody will jump out from behind a seat and start pounding on him. He flops down next to me and takes off his jacket, hitting me in the face while he does it.

I push myself up against the window, trying to get out of his way. He says, "Uh, sorry." Maybe he's retarded, or stoned.

"That's okay." I'm not trying to get into a fight on the first day.

The brothers are sitting just a row behind us. I would have thought they'd sit in the back, but maybe it doesn't work the same way here. They look alike, but one has dark hair and the other has blond hair, and they both have crew cuts.

The one with the blond hair puts his head over the seat and whispers, "Hey, Nat, are you going to ask out Shelley?"

Nat turns around with a disgusted look on his face. I'm guessing Shelley is the girl with the outdated Salvation Army outfit. He says, "Shut up, Billy." There's definitely something wrong with him. Everything he says is twice as slow as it should be.

The dark-haired brother leans his head in on the other side. "Come on, Nat, ask her out."

"Shut up, Bobby." Okay, the twins' names are Billy and Bobby. Classic.

Billy calls across the aisle to Shelley, "Hey, Shelley, Nat likes you. He wants to go out with you."

She turns around with an angry look. "If he likes me, he can tell me himself." Both Billy and Bobby break up laughing. I don't think she can tell that the joke is on her, but she seems much smarter than Nat, at least in the way she talks.

This is obviously something that has happened before, because once the twins start laughing, her face gets red and she pushes her hand up into her hair and scratches at her scalp. It's kind of gross, because a bunch of dandruff comes out.

Bobby says, "Whoa, call Channel Four. There's flurries in Virginia Beach."

Billy cracks up and gives Bobby a high five. "Maybe they'll cancel school."

"That would be sweet."

I sort of want to stick up for Nat and Shelley, but I also don't want to get into a fight on my first day of school. Especially not with twins with matching crew cuts.

9

I'm worried that they're going to start picking on me too. I start thinking up clever comebacks in my mind, in case they want to start something. Maybe something about them being Siamese twins, joined at the head. Sharing the same brain. Which one of you got the brain? Yeah, something like that could work, if I need it.

Billy looks at me and says, "Hey."

"What's up?"

"Do you hunt?" What? Do I hunt? I don't really know what to say. I guess I could lie, but what would be the point of that?

"No."

"Do you fish?" Is this some sort of redneck question-naire?

"No."

"All right, then."

I guess that's the end of the conversation, because Billy turns around and starts pounding on his brother's shoulder.

"Damn, Billy, what you do that for?"

"Wanted to."

"Damn. Quit."

I look out the window and try to judge by the sunlight which direction we're heading. I've gotten confused because of all the commotion with the twins and the mentally in-competent couple, so I can't judge if we're heading north or west at the moment.

Sometimes, when I'm not sure where I am, I try to get my bearings—and for some reason that makes me feel better.

I wonder if that's what the explorers used to do after they'd traveled a long distance in one day; would they double-check and make sure they were heading in the right direction, or would they just continue on the same course? I don't know, I'll have to look that up.

The land is so flat around here, there's nothing to judge the slant of sunlight by. We turn right and then left and then right again. I'm so turned around. I think I've lost my sense of direction completely.

We pull up in front of the school with about twenty other buses all parked at a diagonal to the sidewalk. The driver opens the doors and we all shuffle off into the bright light and warm air.

Okay, so I've already seen six or seven unbelievably beautiful girls, and they're all wearing really short skirts and shirts that reveal their midriffs. I read in the school rules that girls aren't allowed to show their midriffs, but I guess maybe they didn't get that memo. Not that I'm complaining.

The halls are crowded and there's a bottleneck somewhere near the cafeteria. People are trying to push by around the edges, but we have to press our bodies up against the lockers to get by.

There's a really hot girl in front of me—one of the ones who didn't get the memo—and as we push by the bottleneck, I let my hand go limp and my arm swings forward and the back of my hand brushes against her butt. I really wanted to do that. I could almost feel the shape of her ass against my hand. I try again. I let my hand go limp and let it swing forward, letting gravity do the work.

Her ass is so nice. I can even feel her panties through her skirt. Jesus, what an ass. I'm about to do it again when she turns around and gives me the evil eye.

Oops, maybe that wasn't such a good idea. I totally just got busted for being a pervert. I'm such an asshole.

The halls are so crowded that the tides of people going past shove me into my locker. I have to work hard to keep myself pushed away enough so that I can do the combination. The combination is fourteen to the left, twenty-six to the right, twelve to the left. That will be easy to remember, because fourteen plus twelve is twenty-six.

My first class is Latin II, and it's located out behind the school in a trailer. They're doing construction on part of the school and so they have to put us in this trailer.

The teacher introduces himself. He says his name is Mr. Mawson and that he's from South Africa, but I don't get that, because he's a white guy. He's huge. He must be six-six or six-seven, but besides that he has two other defining characteristics. One: He's covered in hair. Not just on his head—he's got hair all over his arms and hands and coming out from under his collar. He already has a five o'clock shadow at seven-thirty a.m. Also, his eyebrows have that brambling-bush look—you know, where they're curling out and away from his face, almost like wings.

The other defining characteristic is his voice. South

African accents sound a little like English accents, except Mr. Mawson's voice is high and grating, like the sound a train makes when it puts on its emergency brake. It's weird because of his size. You'd expect a big guy like that to have a deep voice.

One more thing: He moves around like an ape. You know how apes move, with their arms out and extended almost down to the ground. I swear Mr. Mawson's knuckles practically scrape the ground when he's walking around. Not really, but almost.

No one wants to learn Latin early in the morning—when does anyone want to learn Latin? But in the morning it's a real drag. So Mr. Mawson gets all exaggerated with his gorilla arms, and his train-wreck voice gets even higher, trying to get us interested.

"Right! Ready for Latin, children! LATIN IS FUN! Increases your vocabulary, doesn't it, children? READY? NO GOOD DOGS ATE ANCHOVIES? Right, children? That's Latin!"

I have absolutely no idea what he's talking about, even though I took Latin at my old school. He's making almost no sense.

"Are you paying attention, children? NOTHING GRAMMAR DOES ASTOUNDS AMERICANS, right, children? That's Latin!"

I stare down at my notebook and write my name, because I can't make any sense out of what he's saying.

"NEVER GRAB DEVILS AROUND ANKLES, right, children?"

Now I'm doodling. I turn *Maybe* into a roller coaster. I sketch a track over all the peaks and valleys of the letters.

Mr. Mawson isn't getting a response from anyone—even with his exaggerations—so he starts walking up and down the aisles, shouting the answer as loud as he can. "Right! NOMINATIVE! GENITIVE! DATIVE! ACCUSATIVE! ABLATIVE! Right, children?"

As he passes my desk, he notices my doodling and snatches the notebook off my desk with his gorilla hands.

"What's this, eh?" he shrieks. He holds the notebook up above his head and shows it to the class. "No doodling in Latin, eh? Latin is not doodling."

He drops the notebook onto my desk and continues his lecture, and I try to disappear into my orange plastic chair.

I like movies. I don't know why. There's something about them that clicks with my brain. I love the feeling of being inside a movie theater and looking up at that gigantic screen and the lights going down and all that.

When I'm at a movie, I feel like the things that are going on in my life don't really matter. That's why I signed up for this Visual Language class. I read the course description and it seemed cool. I thought that there would be a whole bunch of artsy people in the class—wannabe filmmakers and painters and photographers—but instead there are just a bunch of lame kids with baseball caps pulled over their eyes.

The teacher, Ms. Haynes, goes into her opening remarks

and takes roll. I'm the only one paying attention. I think everyone else in this class is sleeping.

Except there's this one girl on the other side of the room who seems like she's paying attention too. She's got long red hair, and lots of freckles, like people with red hair have. She's got kind of a pretty face, and she's wearing one of those long hippy dresses that looks like she made it at home, but maybe she just bought it at a store.

Every time I look up at the board, I can see the girl across the room looking at me. It's weird.

I glance up at Ms. Haynes and then right back at the hippy girl. This time I catch her looking at me, but instead of looking away—like any normal person would do—she grins like the Cheshire cat from *Alice in Wonderland*.

Ms. Haynes finally stops talking as the bell rings, and I get my bag and walk across the room. The Cheshire cat hippy girl is waiting for me at the door. I nod at her and she says, "Are you feeling properly edified today?"

I don't know what that means, so I say, "What?"

She must think that I didn't hear her, so she says it again, but a little louder and slower. "Are you feeling properly edified today?"

"What does that mean?"

"Edified?"

"Yeah."

"You take Latin. Figure it out."

"How do you know I take Latin?"

"I'm in your class. Mr. Mawson. You're the doodler."

I hadn't noticed her in that class.

"Oh, right. Well, see you around." I walk out of the class and down the hall toward where I think my next class is going to be.

She follows me down the hall and calls out, "It means educated—taught. It means did you learn enough?" I don't turn around. I just keep walking. I don't know what her deal is.

There are sixteen hundred kids in this high school, and we're all trying to get to different rooms at exactly the same time. We have five minutes to travel, but because there are twice as many kids in the hallways as there should be, no one can actually get to where they're going on time.

We press up against each other—chest to back—and shuffle forward like a millipede in a glue trap.

I'm shuffling behind another hot girl in a short skirt and press my chest against her back. I smell her hair. My fingertips brush against the back of her thighs, which are as smooth as glass. Warm, fleshy glass.

I imagine putting my hands around her and feeling her breasts from behind. I imagine pressing against her butt and kissing her neck.

I can imagine it all, but I know that it probably will never happen.

I walk past a guy and a girl making out in the hallway. I can see his tongue going in and out of her mouth. Why is that guy so lucky, and I'm so unlucky?

I take a detour into the boys' bathroom and take a leak. There are a few other guys pissing too, and we all stand there and stare straight ahead. There are obscene comments written in Magic Marker and a drawing of a dick with a pair of glasses. Whoever drew that needs to take an art class.

All the other guys leave without washing their hands, but I do. My mom always used to yell at my brother and me if we didn't—so I do, out of habit, like putting on my seat belt.

I look in the mirror. My eyes are too far apart and my hair is messy. My skin is breaking out all over the place and my lips are chapped. I forgot to shave and I have this stupid-looking mustache. My brother would say it looks like a caterpillar.

I think I have a monobrow. I also think there's something wrong with my face. I wonder if I got dropped when I was a baby or something, because one side of my face looks like it's lower than the other side.

Does everybody have one eye that goes down on one side, or is it just me? I think it's just me.

Fuck.

I don't eat lunch. I'm not hungry. Instead, I go to the library. Apparently, they let you go in there during your lunch period, as long as you don't have any food.

I put my bag on one of the tables and start walking through the stacks. I like to browse through libraries. I just like the feeling of being around books—I don't know why, I guess it's kind of comforting. Most people forget that whatever you want to know about, you can find it in the library.

I walk by the encyclopedias and run my hand along the spines of the books just to feel their texture. My fingers tingle a little from touching the rough bindings. There's so much to know in the world. I wish I could learn everything in all these books just by touching them. Learn everything in them through osmosis or something. I mean, I know about some things, but then I start thinking about all the things I don't know, and it makes me feel so stupid.

This is what I'm going to do during my lunch period. I'm going to come in here every day and pick an encyclopedia and read as much of it as I can. That's what I'm going to do. I'm going to make a list of everything I want to learn about.

I walk back to the table where my bag is and open it. For some reason there's a book in there already. How did that get here? It's a book about sewing.

I look around the library and I notice a bunch of people at another table. They're looking over at me and laughing.

Oh, I get it. That guy put this sewing book in my bag so when I walked out of here the alarm would go off and I'd get in trouble. What an asshole.

I hate this place. I take the book out of my bag and walk out of the library into the hallway.

There are four or five different security guards at this school. They're hard to miss. They're all really big and built. They wear these shirts with their names on them. I walk past a big guy named Clarence. He says, "Hall pass."

"Sorry?"

"Hall pass. Got to have a hall pass."

"I don't have one. I'm in lunch."

"Can't be wandering the halls."

"Right. Sorry. I'll go back to the library."

"Nope. No can do. Got to have a hall pass."

"Okay, then I'll go to the cafeteria."

"Nope. Got to have a hall pass."

"I don't have one."

"Got to have a hall pass to be in the halls."

"Okay, so what do I do if I don't have a hall pass?"

"Got to have a hall pass to be in the halls."

"Right, I understand, but what I'm saying is that I don't have a hall pass. So I need to be in the halls to go somewhere where I don't need a hall pass."

"Don't get fresh."

"Okay, but do you understand what I'm saying? I need to walk through the halls to be somewhere where I don't need a hall pass. So either you need to let me go this time and I'll never ever go into the halls without a hall pass again, or we can stand here and continue this edifying conversation." I know I'm being fresh, but this is the sort of thing that really gets under my skin—stupid people being stupid for no reason.

"Get out!" He looks like I really pissed him off with my little monologue there. I thought for sure he wouldn't hurt me, because he's a school employee, so I could afford to be a little fresh, but now that I look at his face, I'm not totally sure he's not going to snap into a rage at any moment.

He's pointing toward a door that leads outside. Is he really kicking me out of school? That seems a little weird. Isn't the idea to keep kids in school, or is it really more just about having hall passes and following rules? Clarence answers my question by pointing even more ferociously at the door.

I walk outside. There are a ton of kids out here. I didn't even know we could come out here. That's what he was upset about. I didn't know this was even an option during lunch.

I look around. I don't know anyone. Wait. I see the Cheshire cat hippy girl sitting under a tree with a bunch of other hippy people. One guy has a guitar, and there are two other people—I can't tell what their gender is, because they both have long hair—sitting with them in a circle. God, what year is this, 1967? I didn't even know they still made hippies like this.

Cheshire sees me standing there looking at them and waves to me to come over. I don't have anywhere else to go, so I go over and stand next to her.

"Hey, it's the doodler. Have a seat. Hey, this is the guy I was telling you about."

I say hey to everyone and sit down next to Cheshire.

The guy playing guitar nods and the other two people nod too—one is a boy and one's a girl. I can tell because one has a beard.

Cheshire says, "I never properly introduced myself. I'm Ashley." She puts her hand out. There are yellow stains on the ends of her fingers. She must smoke a lot.

"Hey, I'm Brian."

"Cool. Did you just move here or something?"

"Yeah."

"Are you an army brat?"

"No. Are you?"

"No." She laughs as if the idea is preposterous. "Do I look like an army brat? John, he said I look like an army brat."

John is the guy playing guitar. He doesn't look up from the song he's strumming. It's just the same chords over and over. I don't think he knows any other songs.

I wish I'd never come over here. Now I'm stuck hanging out with people in an awkward social situation. I hate awkward social situations.

Ashley leans over and whispers in my ear, "After school we're all going to go over to John's house and get baked. You wanna come?"

Her eyes are wide open and she wiggles her eyebrows, like a cartoon. This is what I was afraid was going to happen. I knew as soon as I got to school I was going to meet up with people and get offered drugs. I knew this was going to happen.

I shake my head and stand up. "All right, I'll see you guys around." And then I walk back toward the school.

I've never smoked weed. I mean, I would like to try it, but the thing is that I promised my brother I never would. It's not an option.

Ashley runs after me and catches up as I get to the doors of the school. "Sorry, did I offend you?" She has a way of talking that seems extra formal, especially for a girl who is dressed like a hippy. It's almost like she's from another time, or England.

"No, no. It's cool. I just have something to do." I lie because I don't want her to know that I've never smoked weed before.

"Listen, if you're adamant about abstaining from our narcotics, please don't think that means that you're not welcome at our gathering regardless."

"Right, okay. Thanks."

"Great, so you'll come?"

"I will? Okay, I guess I will."

How did I wind up in this situation?

After my last class, I walk down the main hallway toward the buses all parked diagonally in the front of the school. Shit, I don't remember what bus I'm supposed to get on.

Ashley sees me in the hallway and waves. She's been waiting for me, apparently. Well, if I go with her at least I can find my way home.

She leads me to her car, which is a total piece of shit two-door Toyota with Grateful Dead bumper stickers all over the back of the car and on the back windshield. I get in the passenger's seat—I guess John and the hippy twins have their own transportation. The car smells like incense and perfume, and there are coffee cups and cheeseburger wrappers all over the seat. Ashley wipes all of the trash down into the foot-well area and motions for me to get in.

I don't know if this is such a good idea. I mean, what am

I doing getting into a car with a girl I don't know, going over to someone's house I know even less, to sit and watch them do drugs that I don't want anything to do with?

I get in.

Ashley turns on the tape player. It's some techno thing with a beat that could only be created by a computer. It's so repetitive, but Ashley seems like she's into it. She's nodding her head with the beat, which makes her look like a robot with a short circuit.

She drives too fast, passing people on the right on the four-lane road. I'm not used to the roads around here. Every road has at least two lanes each way, and a lot of the main roads have four lanes going each way. What is that? It must be a Southern thing.

Ashley slips in and out of traffic and then turns in to a neighborhood. She parks on the street in front of a run-down little house with aluminum siding.

She turns to me and says, "We've arrived."

I get out and bring my book bag with me—I don't know why I'm bringing it. It's not like we're going to be doing homework, but on the other hand, I don't want it to get stolen. Although, on the third hand, whoever lives in this neighborhood probably isn't going to be stealing books.

We go right into the house. It's really dark in here. The blinds are pulled down and no one has bothered to turn on a light. There's smoke in the air already, and it's drifting in the light that has slipped through the blinds, like the fog in *Hound of the Baskervilles*.

John and the hippy twins are sitting in chairs around the

room. It looks like they're each holding a small piece of wood and a knife. Are they whittling? What the hell is going on?

Ashley says, "Hey, guys, got your projects out already? What an engaged and prolific group of drug addicts you are." She flops down on the couch and I sit next to her, because there's nowhere else to sit.

She says, "We're carving our own bowls. John's making a lion. Mine is a dolphin."

Bowls? They look more like pipes than anything else. I say that out loud.

Ashley looks at me and laughs, and the rest of the group starts laughing too. She says, "Oh, you sweet and naive child. Bowl is another word for pipe."

I didn't know that. Now I feel stupid. Ashley says, "Who's got something for me to smoke?" John hands her a small wooden pipe and a lighter, and she puts it in her mouth. She lights the lighter with the index finger of her hand and sways it back and forth over the end of the pipe. She takes a deep breath and holds the smoke in her lungs, then smiles at me with her Cheshire cat smile and lets the smoke drift out from between her teeth.

She offers me the pipe and I shake my head. She raises her eyebrows as if to say, Suit yourself, and then puts the pipe back in her mouth and takes another drag. She talks and inhales at the same time. "Gotta play catch-up."

I look at how the fire changes the color of her face. She does have a pretty face. She's a little overweight, though. Maybe more than a little.

I wonder if she'll let me have sex with her. Probably not.

Everyone is quiet while Ashley keeps smoking. She takes a few more hits and then says, "John, got any Chapstick?"

For some reason this is the funniest thing that anyone in the room has ever heard. They laugh, and keep laughing, and keep laughing even longer. What is the deal? What she said wasn't funny, or if it was, then I don't get it.

I wait for them to stop laughing, and say, "What's so funny about Chapstick?"

This starts them all laughing again, except John. He's not laughing. He's just staring at me.

I stare back at him, because I don't know why he's staring at me. When Ashley stops laughing finally, John says, "He's cute. Is he gay?" Shit, do I look gay?

Ashley says, "I don't know. Ask him yourself."

John looks me up and down and says, "Are you gay?" No one has ever asked me if I'm gay before. Are people wondering all the time whether or not I'm gay?

"No. I'm not gay."

"Are you at least bi?"

"No."

"That's too bad."

Wow. God, I hope I don't look gay. Do I look gay?

I mean, obviously I'm not gay, because I've never had sex with a man, but I've never had sex with a woman either, so does that mean I'm not straight? Am I bisexual?

Jesus, what if I'm bisexual? What would my parents say? I bet they'd kill me.

I wonder what he would have done if I'd said I was gay. Is he gay? I bet he is gay, just by the way he holds himself and the way he talks and stuff. I bet if I'd said that I was gay he would have taken me into the back room and had sex with me right here.

Does it mean that I'm gay because I just had that thought? I mean, the one thing in the world that I want more than anything is to have sex. I just want to have sex with someone. That's all I want. I don't want to die a virgin.

I wonder if I'm getting high off all these fumes in here. It smells like a small burning forest, and there's definitely some secondhand-smoke stuff going on right about now. I don't think I feel different, but I can't really tell.

I wonder where John's parents are. Does he have parents? Do they care that he sits around in the living room and smokes weed after school?

I look up at the ceiling fan. Wow, that thing is going around so slowly. I wonder whether it's on or if some wind is pushing it. No, the smoke is just sitting around in the room, so there's no wind, so it must be on. But if it's on, why is there no wind?

Look at that tapestry hanging on the wall. It looks like it's breathing. Look at how it's going in and out—like it's on a respirator.

They're playing some music too. The music is slow and it matches up perfectly with the air in the room and the smoke and the tapestry inhaling and exhaling.

Wow. I think I'm getting high off this shit. Fuck. I promised my brother I was never going to do this. This is bullshit. I've got to get out of here.

I stand up. Ashley looks up at me. "Where are you going?"

"I need to go home. I just remembered."

"Chill. We're not going anywhere."

"I have to. I have to go. Get up. You need to drive me."

"Honey, I'm not driving anywhere."

"You have to. I have to go. I'm serious. Get up."

She stands up as slowly as a person can without falling back down again. She picks up her bag and moves like a sloth to the front door, which I'm holding open for her. She turns around and says, "See you guys later."

Her eyes are half-closed and red. Jesus, she probably shouldn't drive, but on the other hand, I have to get out of this opium-den situation. I take her keys and open the passenger door for her. I'm such a gentleman.

She slides into the seat and rests her head against the headrest. I look down her dress. She's not wearing a bra—that's kind of hot. I can see where her breasts start. She's got freckles all over her chest—that's too bad, but still, she's a girl and I'm kind of attracted to her. I wonder if she'll let me have sex with her. At least that would mean that I'm not gay.

I still have to solve the problem of getting myself home. The first part of the problem is that I don't have a driver's license. I do have a learner's permit—that's something—but if I get pulled over by a cop, I'm going to lose my license forever.

On the other hand, I can't let Ashley drive me home. She's so high she can barely keep her eyes open. If she drives we'll probably crash and die—but I'm not staying here with the drug addicts. That's insane.

I guess I could call my parents at work, but what am I going to tell them? I just went over to a friend's house and sat around while they got high and now I need a ride home? That's not going to go over well.

I take a few deep breaths and try to push the leftover drug smoke out of my lungs. I adjust the seat and adjust the mirrors, just like I'm supposed to, and then I start the car. This car really is a piece of shit. Ashley pops out the techno tape and puts in some hippy tape with a mandolin.

I check for other cars and then put it into drive and head for the stop sign that leads to the main road. I put my left turn signal on about five hundred feet before the intersection. I come to a complete stop right before the white line painted on the street and then check the traffic going both ways.

There aren't any cars, so I can probably go. I look both ways again, just to be safe. Okay. No cars. I should go. I check once more just to be triply safe, and I pull out into the intersection. Fuck, I'm driving on a road without a license with a hippy girl I hardly know who's high as a kite.

I say, "Ashley, you're high as a kite, huh?"

For some reason this starts her singing some song I've

never heard before, but I recognize the melody from the song John was playing on the guitar at lunch.

*"When I'm out walking I strut my stuff yeah I'm so strung out. I'm high as a kite I just might stop to check you out."*

"What's that?" I say.

" 'Blister in the Sun.' "

"Right." Gross.

I put my blinker on and get into the right lane. I'm driving slow, probably too slow, because everyone is passing me.

The road has four lanes going each way, and everybody, for some reason, is changing lanes all the time. I don't know if they're trying to get over to make a turn, or if they're just trying to get wherever they're going faster.

I hope we don't get pulled over. If we get pulled over I'm totally going to be screwed for life. I keep checking my mirrors and the speedometer to make sure I'm not going too fast. The speed limit is forty-five and I'm going about thirty-five.

Ashley is spacing out, looking at something out the window.

I'm getting a little more comfortable with the whole driving thing. I mean, everything in this town is just straight and flat anyway, so it's not like there are too many obstacles.

We pull up to a red light and I put my foot on the brake and stop behind a Honda. I look over at Ashley and she looks back at me. She's kind of attractive; you know, she's got a pretty face and she's smart. I could see myself having sex with her. I wonder if I get her to come inside the house if she'll have sex with me. Who knows, maybe she will since she's high.

I turn right onto Lynnhaven and right again onto Smith. This road is so empty and straight. I push down the gas pedal and the crappy little Toyota gets a boost. The inertia pushes Ashley and me back in our seats a little, and she turns her head and starts paying attention.

"What are you doing?" she says.

"Nothing."

"Well, slow down."

I don't want to slow down. I want to go as fast as possible. I want to go until the wheels lift off the ground and the car flies off the road.

I'm scaring myself. I don't want to do this. I take my foot off the gas and let the car coast back to a normal speed. She says, "What was that?"

"Nothing."

"Okay, well, don't do that again, okay?"

"Okay." I just wanted to see how fast the car would go, because the road was so straight and there was no one ahead of us. I just wanted to see how fast it would go.

I turn left at the stop sign and through the S curves to my house. I park in the driveway. She looks up and says, "This is your house? Impressive."

"Yeah, I guess." I look up at it. It is kind of huge, but I'm not sure it's really impressive. It's big and brick and on a kind of swampy river; maybe that is impressive.

I turn off the car but don't take off my seat belt. I don't

know why. I just have a feeling, like we're going to be sitting here for a while.

She looks at me and raises one eyebrow. "I thought you said you had to be home."

"I did."

"So?"

"So now I'm home."

"Isn't someone awaiting your arrival?"

"No, both my parents are at work. They won't be home for hours."

"Hmm," she says, and raises her eyebrow higher.

"Do you wanna come in?" I try to make the invitation sound harmless, like I'm not going to try to jump her bones as soon as she gets in there.

"Hmm." She pauses, and it takes about a hundred and fifty years for her to finish her answer. "No, but I'll sit out here with you for a while."

"Wanna go for a swim? I've got a pool." The pool will do it. She's got to go for the pool thing.

"Nah. Don't have a swimsuit."

"Doesn't matter. You don't need one."

"You're fresh." I didn't actually mean that she would have to go naked, although now that I think about it, I guess that is what it sounded like. I meant we might have an extra swimsuit she could wear—or she could borrow a T-shirt to swim in.

"I didn't mean it like that."

"Right," she laughs. "You're a horny little guy, aren't you?"

Maybe it's just me, but I bet most guys don't like to be called little by girls they're trying to seduce.

I don't answer her question with words; instead, I lean over and tilt my head and close my eyes and do my best to kiss her on her lips. She moves her mouth at the last moment, so all I get is a bunch of cheek.

Because my seat belt is still on, I'm leaning over in a weird way and I have to bring my left arm up and around her body to try and get a good kiss in. She's moving, dodging my kiss, and her body twists to the right and her breast falls into my hand. I'm totally horny.

I'm not really thinking, and I give it a little squeeze. She pushes my hand away and laughs. "Not so fast, bub."

All I want to do is have sex with her. Right here. Right now. I don't care if it's in the car, or in the house, or whatever. It doesn't matter. I'm sixteen years old. I just really need to have sex.

I try again to kiss her, but she pulls away again and says, "Stop," as if she's saying it to a dog that's trying to hump her leg. The thing that's confusing, though, is that she's also smiling. I mean, there must be some part of her that wants me to kiss her.

I pull back and look at her face. I'm trying to figure out what she means. Does she mean stop, like I'm not interested in you, get out of my car? Or does she mean stop, like wait awhile and try again? She's still smiling at me.

I say, "Do you want to come inside?"

"I think that would be an extraordinarily bad idea."

"Why?"

"Because if I come inside I'll probably wind up having sex with you."

"So? What's wrong with that?"

"I'm not sure our relationship is ready for that. I just met you today." When she says relationship, I wonder if she means a boyfriend/girlfriend kind of thing, or if she just means friends who have sex the first day they meet.

I say, "What do you mean?"

"Well, I do want to have sex with you, just so you know."

"Okay. Let's go."

"Wait, I need to know how you feel about me first."

"What do you mean?"

"Do you even like me? Do you want to be my boyfriend? Or are you just looking for a quick fuck?"

"Uh . . ." I don't know what to say. I didn't know this was going to turn into a negotiation. Actions speak louder than words.

I put my hand on top of her hand and slide my fingers through hers. I lean over much slower this time and close my eyes. She lets me kiss her softly on the lips. She tastes like cherry-flavored Chapstick. She slides her tongue into my mouth, like a slippery little worm. I put my tongue into her mouth too, and they swirl around each other. That feels good.

I put my hand on her lap and then onto her stomach and slide it slowly up to her breast. Okay, this is going well. Only about three more minutes of this and we'll be having sex.

As soon as I get a good grip on her breast, she pulls back and says, "Stop," again.

I stop. This is getting ridiculous. Is she going to let me have sex with her or not?

I'm pretty sure there's almost no blood left in my brain. I'm running in all-or-nothing sex mode. I think she knows she's torturing me, because she's got this huge smile on her face again. I'm not smiling. I thought this was supposed to be fun.

She says, "So do you want to go out with me?"

"Um . . ." I can't believe she remembered that she asked that question. I totally forgot about it. I close my eyes and try to understand what's going on here. She'll have sex with me if I agree to go out with her, to be her boyfriend. So basically all I have to say is that I'll be her boyfriend, and then she'll have sex with me. Okay, that should be pretty easy.

Except that I don't really want to be her boyfriend. I mean, I don't really know her that well, and I've seen a lot of things today that I don't really like.

I think she's pretty, but I can't be going out with a girl who smokes weed. My brother would hate that.

So the answer is no, but I still want to have sex with her. I lean over and try to kiss her again, but this time she doesn't even let me do that.

She says, "You have to answer my question."

"Oh . . . okay. I think you should come inside and have sex with me."

"That wasn't the question."

"Right, uh, what was the question?"

"Do you want to be my boyfriend?"

"Uh . . . can I have sex with you and decide later?"

"No."

"Uh . . . can you just come inside and we'll talk about it in there?"

"No, we need to talk about it here."

"Uh . . . do you want to just do some stuff and not have sex and then we can decide about the boyfriend/girlfriend thing later?"

"Hold on."

She unbuckles her seat belt and turns her body so she's facing me in the seat. She looks me right in the eyes and says, "Close." I close my eyes, because that's what she's telling me to do. She puts her hand over my mouth and says, "Open." I open my mouth. I don't know what she's going to do, but I think it has something to do with kissing.

She leans over and kisses me, and at the same time she takes in a deep breath while our lips are together and it's like she's pulling the air right out of my lungs. It's like she put a vacuum cleaner down my throat and sucked all the air right out of me. My eyes are still closed. It feels like dying.

I take a deep breath and get the air back into my lungs. I open my eyes and look at her again. She says, "How was that?"

"Weird."

She shows me her teeth and says, "Has anyone ever done that to you before?"

"No. Where'd you learn that?"

"A friend."

I lean over and try the same thing on her. She lets me suck the air out of her, and it's even weirder to be on the other side of it. I'm sucking the breath from her insides right into mine. I think I can taste the smoke. And her air is hotter than mine for some reason.

I try to kiss her again, but she says, "Stop."

"What?"

"I can't do this here."

"So come inside. We can go into my brother's room." Shit. Where did that come from? I shouldn't have mentioned my brother. I don't want to talk about him.

"You have a brother? Is he home?"

"No."

"Where is he, college?"

"No."

"How old is he?"

I don't say anything else, because I don't want to talk about him. It was a mistake even to bring him up. I shouldn't have done that and I don't know why I did.

Because I'm not answering, she's getting uncomfortable. I look around the car. The windows are all steamed up from our carbon dioxide and our body heat.

I'm sick of sitting in this car with this girl. I don't want to go out with her. I don't even like her. I just wanted to have sex. What's wrong with that?

My balls are aching and I'm tired of this. I say, "Well,

okay, I'm going to go inside. Bye." I unbuckle my seat belt, open the car door, and start to get out.

She grabs my arm and says, "Wait, what just happened?"

"Nothing. I've got to go."

"What do you mean? Did I say something to upset you? Are you okay?"

"I'm fine. It's no big deal. I've got to go. My parents are going to be home any second."

"But you said they wouldn't be home for hours."

"I was wrong. They're going to be home soon. I've got to go inside."

"Okay. Bye."

"Bye."

I walk up to the garage and open the door with one hand. I'm so pissed right now. I go into the bathroom that's right off the garage and take a leak.

There's a mirror right in front of me that I look in while I'm pissing. I have three words in my head that are repeating, and I don't know why. Three words that are repeating—broken-record style—inside my brain. I hate this. I hate this. I hate this.

My parents come home and we eat dinner together. Dad sits at one end of the table and I sit at the other end. Mom sits on the right side, and the chair on the other side of the table is empty.

Dad says, "How was the first day of school, son?"

"Fine."

Mom says, "How were your classes?"

"Fine."

"Did you make any friends?"

I think about that one for a second. I don't know if Ashley is my friend or if I can't stand her. I sort of feel both ways about it. I say, "Maybe."

# THREE

It's Saturday. I'm so tired. I'm so tired of waking up at six in the morning and going to school. I'm sleeping as late as possible. I'm going to lie in bed forever and never wake up.

I'm not going to open my eyes. I'm just going to lie here and think about that dream I was just having. I was in an old house with a bunch of people I didn't know. It was a party, I guess, and I was walking around through the different rooms and I was looking for someone, but I can't remember who I was looking for.

I woke up with the loneliest feeling. I feel like no one knows me and no one even wants to know me.

I open my eyes and look at the red digital clock next to my bed. It's eleven-thirty. I slept for a dozen hours. That's weird, because I still feel tired. I wish it had been a baker's dozen.

I go downstairs to get a bowl of cereal for myself and sit in front of the TV. Dad is outside mowing the lawn—that used to be my brother's chore. I think that was what woke me up.

I pour my cereal into the bowl and splash the milk over it. I get some of it on the coffee table, but I don't care.

I flip through the channels, but nothing's on. Maybe I'll watch a movie. I could watch *The Godfather* again, or *The Graduate*. Those are probably my two favorite movies. I look at my movie collection and try to think of something I might want to watch.

I've seen everything I own about two hundred times. I could watch *Reservoir Dogs* again, but I'm not really in the mood. I'm not in the mood for anything, not even *Animal House*.

Mom comes in and stands in front of the TV. I keep staring at it, like she's not there—like I can see right through her.

She says something. I wish I had X-ray vision so I could watch TV while she's standing in front of it. I remember in the back of *Boys' Life* magazine there were all these products you could buy if you collected enough points or something; I always wanted the X-ray glasses so I could see through women's clothes.

Mom turns off the TV because I'm ignoring her, but I just keep staring at it, like it's still on and I'm still watching whatever was even on there.

She says, "Dad needs help with the pool."

I don't say anything, I just look out the window at the pool. Dad is standing out there looking at the water, which was clear when we first moved in, but now it's kind of cloudy and slightly green.

I don't want to help with the pool. I don't want to do anything. I just want to sit here and watch TV and not think about anything at all.

She keeps standing there and puts her hand on her hip, which is the international sign for Get your ass off the couch.

I stand up and go outside.

Dad sees me and waves. He says, "Wanna help with the pool?"

"Not really."

He scowls, but he doesn't say anything. He reaches down into the water and fills a little container. He says, "There's something wrong with it. I don't know what it is."

I almost say, I know what's wrong with it. You don't know what the hell you're doing. But I don't.

He says, "I've gotta go to the pool store and find out what's wrong with the water." He looks at me like he's about to ask if I want to come too, but he doesn't ask. He just takes his container of pool water, gets in the car, and drives away.

I'm glad he didn't ask. I'm going back to bed.

# fOUR

Chorus sucks. I just stand on the riser with the two other guys and mumble through the songs. It's not like it matters. It's not like people are listening to me. I'm sure that no one can even hear me, because I'm hardly making any noise at all.

Everything that comes out of my mouth sounds so stupid.

There's this one girl in the alto section who can sing her ass off. She's by far the best one in the whole class, and she's not even trying. She just opens up her mouth and these amazing, beautiful sounds come out.

I watch her from the back row of the risers. She's

got long brown hair that comes down to the middle of her back. She has brown eyes too. She's not skinny and she doesn't have the best complexion, but when she opens her mouth to sing she is the most attractive girl I've ever seen.

She is the only good thing about being in Chorus.

My second-to-last class of the day is U.S. History. The teacher, Mrs. Humphrey, is a real Southern lady. She has this thick accent that I can hardly understand. She is talking about how our nation is not really a melting pot but more of a salad bowl. She says, "You see, we're more of a salad. Made up of very individual and distinct pieces in the same general area. We have lettuce—maybe some iceberg lettuce—and some tomatoes—vine-ripened."

I don't understand what she's talking about. I can't tell if the different parts of the salad are supposed to be metaphors for different races of people or if she is really just listing ingredients for salad. Maybe lettuce is white people and tomatoes are black people? I don't know. I'm trying to figure it out, but she just keeps listing ingredients, like this is a cooking class. "We have cucumbers. We have olives."

Maybe cucumbers are the English? Olives—Italians?

"We have a nice vinegar dressing."

Who is that supposed to be? I am so totally lost in her salad metaphor.

"And of course we have the Spanish."

Oh my God, did she just say Spanish, or did she say spinach? Oh my God, please tell me she didn't just say Spanish.

I put my head down and laugh into my loose-leaf binder.

# fIVE

I've been trying to avoid Ashley during lunch, but it's kind of difficult. I already see her in my first two classes, and she's always talking to me and asking if I want to hang out and stuff, but the thing is that I don't really want to hang out with her. I mean, she's okay, but it's just that whole drug thing I can't deal with.

Today, instead of going to the library to avoid her, I go and hang out in the theater. The place is empty, except for a few theater geeks up onstage. I sit in the back and read a book. It's pretty comfortable, actually, sitting in here. It's air-conditioned and no one bothers me.

The theater geeks are all acting ridiculous and running around playing tag or something. They're just like little kids.

A guy with red hair and a backward baseball hat walks in through the back door and across the stage. All the kids who were joking around and laughing stop and watch him enter, but he doesn't even acknowledge them. He seems like he's above it all. I wish I could get people to look at me like that.

He walks up the aisle toward me. Shit, I knew I shouldn't have come in here. I knew I was making a mistake, but I'm not even doing anything—I'm just reading my book.

The guy walks right up to where I am and sits down at the end of the row and puts his feet up on the seat in front of him. Now I can't get out. He's blocking me in.

He takes out a brown paper bag with his lunch in it. He must eat here every day or something. Shit, I must have accidentally stumbled into his territory. I knew I shouldn't have come in here.

He takes out an apple and a bag of Cheetos from his lunch and then looks over at me, like he just now noticed that I've been sitting here, and says, "You hungry?"

"Huh?"

"I've got some extra stuff in my lunch—if you want it."

"Yeah, thanks."

"I'm Dan."

"Brian."

He says, "Only Thespians are allowed to eat in the theater. So you're going to have to eat this in the hall." He hands me the apple from his lunch.

"You sure you don't want it?"

"I'm sure. My mom packs me all this shit. I don't know why. I think she's trying to fatten me up for the kill."

I laugh, take the apple from him, and go out into the hall. I take a big bite and look back in at him sitting there eating his Cheetos, above it all, not giving a shit about anybody. I wish I could be like that.

My Chemistry teacher, Mr. Thompson, is a Marine, and he talks all the time like he's a drill sergeant. What's weird is, everyone in the class answers all of his questions like we're his cadets. I don't know how that happened, but I think it's kind of funny.

He says, "What's the first element on the periodic table?"

"Hydrogen, sir."

"How many protons does it have?"

"One, sir."

I'm having a really hard time figuring out the gist of Chemistry, though. I missed a class last week, because I was sick, and that was the day of the big test—so I have to stay after school today and make it up.

Mr. Thompson hands out everyone else's Scantron, and I look over this girl's shoulder who sits in front of me. She understands everything. She got a 97 on the test, which means she only missed one. God, I wish I had her brain.

When the bell rings I follow her out of the class and walk behind her in the hallway. I tap her on the shoulder and say, "Hey."

She turns around like she's afraid I'm going to attack her and says, "Hey."

"Do you have that test from Chemistry?"

"Yeah."

"Can I see it?"

"Why?"

"I just want to use it to study. I have to take the test after school today."

"Uh, but it's a Scantron. It doesn't have the questions, only the answers."

"That's okay."

"Okay, but don't get caught with this—it's got my name on it."

"Okay. I'll give it back after class tomorrow."

She hands me the Scantron and I put it in my folder. During Algebra, U.S. History, and English, I stare at the answers and memorize them. There are only forty-seven questions—and it's multiple choice, so I can remember them pretty easily if I think of them like phrases and not just letters.

ACDB ABBCA BDCBAA DAC DCBA. CCBA DACB BACCD DACAB . . .

I make up a little song to go along with the phrases, and the letters start to make a groove in my memory so that the right letters seem to want to go after each other.

I take the stupid Scantron test after school, and I make sure that I take enough time with the questions so it doesn't seem like I've just memorized the answers.

School is such a waste of time.

# SIX

**D**an has been picking me up and driving me to school every morning, ever since we became friends. He beeps the horn and I run out. I can hear the music as I get closer to the car. It's really loud and angry. From outside the car it sounds just like a guy screaming as loud as he can.

Dan is an actor, and he always wears the same black baseball hat. He wears it backward, which is the way I like to wear my hats, when I wear them. Dan wears a hat because he was in this play over the summer and he had to shave his head for his part, and his hair is growing back funny.

I get in the car and put on my seat belt. I have to wear a

seat belt. My mother is a crazy seat-belt person. Ever since I was little, she always told me and my brother to put our seat belts on every time we got in the car—even if we were just driving from one parking space to another in front of the supermarket.

Anyway, I'm glad I'm wearing my seat belt, because Dan is driving really fast. He's taking every turn like he's trying to break the land speed record, and the car feels like it might flip, so I grab the handle on the ceiling and hold on.

Dan seems unconcerned. Actually, he seems more concerned with the music on the stereo. Dan's got a thing where he can't listen to an entire song. He listens to the beginning of a song, and sometimes the middle, but never the end. It's like he's always chasing after that brilliant moment where the guitar is loudest and the singer is screaming, and after that he loses interest. I can relate to that.

Instead of going left on Lynnhaven, like we would if we were going to school, Dan makes a right. I want to ask him where he's going, but the music is so loud that I don't think he'll hear me. He pulls in to the gas station, takes off his seat belt, and opens the door, but before he gets out he turns to me and says, "Got any money?"

"Huh? Yeah, I've got a couple of bucks."

"Give it."

"Oh, okay." I dig into my pocket and give him the two bucks I was saving for lunch. Dan pumps the gas and puts two bucks' worth into the car. I wonder what would've happened if I hadn't had any money.

He gets back into the car and drives fast out of the

parking lot. Dan makes a left onto Virginia Beach Boulevard, which is eight lanes, four going each way. He swerves from the far left lane into the far right lane without checking his blind spot or using his blinker and speeds up as he heads toward a red stoplight.

I'm pretty sure that red means stop and green means go, so I don't know why he's speeding toward a red light, but at the last second the light changes from red to green and we go right through.

Dan says, "Chill." I didn't even notice I was doing this, but I guess I had my foot pressed down on the imaginary brake pedal on my side of the car. That's weird, because that's exactly what my mom used to do when she took Sean out for driving lessons and he started driving too fast.

There's another car pulling up alongside us. It's an old blue Volvo station wagon, the kind with the rear seat that faces backward. My family used to have one of those. I can remember fighting with my brother over who was going to get to sit in the back on long car trips. Most of the time he won, because he was bigger—unless I cried about it, and then I got to sit back there.

The blue Volvo pulls in front of us and I get a good look at the backseat. There's a teenager sitting in the seat. I think it's a boy, but he's got long blond hair like a girl. He must be a surfer. He's smoking something—a cigarette? No, that doesn't look like a cigarette, because he's passing it to another long-haired surfer dude, in the second row of seats. I think they're smoking a joint on the way to school. That's not going to help the GPA.

Dan yanks the car over into the left lane and guns it. We inch up past their front bumper, and then Dan turns his signal on and makes a hard left turn onto a road called North Great Neck.

"Shortcut," he says.

Everything around here is Necks—Great Neck, Little Neck. I swear I've seen a sign on a building that says LITTLE NECK MASSAGE CENTER. Seriously, how funny is that?

The Volvo follows us onto North Great Neck and passes us again, this time on the right.

Dan speeds up again and tries to pass, but we get caught behind another car—another red Honda Civic, newer than the one Dan is driving.

I can see the school sticker on the car, but whoever is driving it—a girl with long blond hair—is not racing.

She's singing with her friend; they're swaying their heads back and forth.

Dan pulls in to the right lane and passes them. The girls look over at us as we pass, and they start laughing. Are they laughing at us?

Finally, we get to school, and we park near the auditorium, a few spaces away from the blue Volvo. The surfer guys are still sitting in there.

Dan walks a few steps ahead of me and I hurry to catch up. It's not that we're late, it's just that we like to hang out with the other theater people before school starts.

Dan is pretty much the man in the theater department. He's starred in almost every play over the last year or so, except for the musical. That's why it's good to be his friend, because all of a sudden everyone here knows me and knows my name.

Everyone sits down in the front of the theater, on the rail in front of the orchestra pit.

Ms. Hanson, the Drama teacher, walks in and says hello to everyone. She's about forty, with curly blond hair, and she's always wearing long black dresses. She looks a little like Bernadette Peters. She has a tattoo of a star and a crescent moon on the back of her neck. People like to talk about her. They say that she's a witch, an actual witch. People also say that sometimes she sleeps with her students, but that can't be true, because she's married and has a son.

The rumor is that she invites a guy over to her house for a spaghetti dinner and then she seduces him. I wonder if that's true. Dan is supposed to be one of the people she seduced.

Everyone brought their breakfasts with them and they're all eating. Wally is eating a bagel with cream cheese. Sid has a bag full of Dunkin' Donuts Munchkins he's throwing up in the air and catching in his mouth. Cheryl is eating hash browns from McDonald's.

All of these people are Thespians, except for me. The Thespians is a special club for the theater people. To join, you have to go through this thing called Plebe Week, where you have to wear a stupid beanie all day in school and ask permission to speak. Everyone keeps asking me if I'm going to plebe, because I'm one of the only ones who hasn't. Dan says that if I plebe, he'll be my sponsor and he'll make it easy on me, so I think that I'm going to do it.

The thing I'm worried about is the last night of Plebe Week. People talk about it, but no one says what really happens. All they'll say is that everyone is confronted with their worst fears on Induction Night; I'm not sure I'm ready for that.

But after it's over, you're a Thespian for life and you can eat in the theater.

# SEVEN

It's only a few weeks into the school year, and already I know that taking Chorus was the worst mistake of my entire life. I wish there had been auditions for this. Then someone would have told me that I can't sing. It's so embarrassing. First of all, there are only two other guys in the class and fourteen girls, and the girls all sing so loud that I can't even hear myself. The girls' singing gets in my head and then I start to try to sing what they're singing and it doesn't turn out that well.

Shit. It's so embarrassing. Not to mention the fact that we have to go out and sing in other schools and shit. Why did I get involved in this? What is wrong with me? My guidance counselor suggested it and then I, like an idiot, decided to go along with the whole thing. Seriously, is there something wrong with me?

We got measured for our outfits today. Oh my God. Let's just say that a sequined vest is not my idea of a fashionable outfit.

Maybe I am just an idiot who does what other people want him to do. Maybe that's my problem. Maybe I should have told Mr. Scott I didn't want to be in Chorus or Shop and that I wanted to be in a Theater class, but I'm not that gutsy. I'm just not.

Mrs. Boone is sitting at the piano, warming us up. She makes us do this exercise. She hits a key on the piano and we all sing. "One, one, one. One, two, three. One, two, three, four, five. One, eight, five, three. Five, four, three, two, one."

I get messed up on the one, eight, five, three part, because she keeps looking at me and shaking her head. She says, "Eight is the same note as one, just up an octave."

I don't know what an octave is. I don't understand. How is eight the same as one?

I close my eyes and try to hear myself. It's hard, though, with all these other people singing at the same time. I close my eyes to try and hear what it is that is coming out of my mouth, but I can't hear anything. All I can hear is the other people.

When I open my eyes, I see the girl with the beautiful voice looking at me from the alto section. Why is she looking at me? She's probably wondering why I'm even in this class. She definitely knows why eight and one are the same thing.

Why is she looking at me? Does she think I'm stupid? Is she making fun of me? Does she wish I would just disappear and never come back into this room again?

I can't tell what she's thinking—all I know is that she's looking at me, and that is not an altogether bad feeling. Mrs. Boone says, "Katya, will you help Brian with some of the basics?"

She says, "Sure." Her name is Katya. What a name.

Katya is walking over. Oh my God, I don't know what to say to her.

She says, "How's it going?"

I say, "Sort of terribly, to be honest."

She laughs a little. "I know what you mean." She looks me right in the eye. Her eyes are this dark brown color with flecks of green and gold, and she looks like she feels sorry for me.

She takes me off into the corner and says, "Here, listen. One, three, five, eight. One, eight. One, eight. Hear that?"

"No. Not really? What do you mean?"

"You know how notes have letters? A, B, C, D, E, F, and G?"

"Yeah, I guess." I sort of remember that from elementary-school music.

"Well, if A is one, the next time you get to A it's eight. You see?"

"Oh, right. Okay. So eight and one are both A?"

"Yeah, basically. You got it."

"Okay. Thanks."

"No problem." She walks back to her section and smiles at me again.

My last class is English—not Honors English or AP English, just English. Our teacher was supposed to be this woman, but I guess she's sick or having a baby, so we have this long-term substitute named Mr. Nestor. He's just a guy out of college. I don't think he's ever even had a teaching job before, or any job. He's so nervous and uncertain about everything he's doing. It kind of makes me laugh.

I don't know why, but he looks to me like his name is Bob. He introduced himself as Mr. Nestor, but I bet his first name is Bob. I bet if I call him Bob he'll respond to it.

He's talking about *The Scarlet Letter* and how he was going to have us read it, but instead we're going to watch a movie of it. I figured it would be the one with Gary Oldman and Demi Moore, but it's not. It's some crappy PBS version with the world's worst lighting. Wow, that is so lame. The acting is, like, sickeningly bad.

I raise my hand. Mr. Nestor comes over to me. I say, "Hey, Bob, do you think we could get a good version of this movie?"

Some of the other kids around me laugh a little when I call him Bob. He says, "What do you mean?"

"Uh, listen, Bob. This has to be the worst version of this movie ever."

The kids around me laugh again. This is great.

I keep going. "Can't we get the Demi Moore version? I mean, I'll go rent it at Blockbuster if I have to. This is terrible, Bob."

Everyone in my whole section is paying attention now. No one's paying attention to this stupid movie. I mean, I appreciate that we don't have to read the book, but this is so stupid.

Bob says, "I can only show movies that have been approved by the school board, so, sorry, can't do it."

"Well, that's a real shame, Bob, because this movie is terrible."

"Your concern is duly noted."

"Thanks, Bob. I appreciate it."

He looks me in the eye like he wants to strangle me for a second and then goes in the back and sits at his permanent-substitute desk. I can't believe I just got away with that.

I know I shouldn't hang out with Ashley, because I don't really like her that much and I think that she likes me a lot, but I can't help it. I keep hoping that if I hang out with her for long enough that she'll let me have sex with her, or at least feel her up or something.

I'm sure if Dan were here he'd already have had sex with her and left. How does he do that?

We're at her house in her room, which is covered in tapestries, and she's burning incense like crazy. She smoked some pot a while ago and now she's lying on her bed listening to Pink Floyd.

I really don't know what I'm doing here. Yes I do. I want

to have sex. That's all I care about. I just want to have sex with someone.

I think Ashley's asleep. She's just lying there on her back with her arms over her head.

One of the things I really like about Ashley is that she doesn't wear underwear. She told me today, she never wears a bra and she only wears panties when she needs to. I'm not sure what she means by that, but I don't want to ask.

Maybe it's the pot that Ashley smoked, or the incense or something, but I'm feeling pretty weird right now.

It's weird. Sometimes when I'm walking around in my house, I think I hear my brother in the next room. I don't know why I think that, because I know he's not there. He's never been in this house, so it's not like a memory. But I still think about him and imagine that he's in the kitchen getting a glass of milk or putting his hamper in the laundry room.

I'm so sure he's there that when I walk into the room and he's not, I get mad. I just get so fucking mad about it.

God damn it. Why am I thinking about that? I shouldn't be thinking about that right now. I should be thinking about how to seduce Ashley.

That's what I should be thinking about. She's lying there with her eyes closed. I wonder if she's asleep.

I think she is. I think she is asleep.

She's kind of sleeping with her legs open a little. The jeans shorts she's wearing are puffed up around her thighs and she's not wearing any underwear. That's so cool. I wonder if I can see anything.

I put my head down near the end of the bed and look up her shorts. I'm not sure exactly what I'm looking for, but I can't really see anything. Is there a flashlight around here? I know she's got a lighter, but I don't think that would be such a good idea.

It's just really dark up there. I'm not even sure what I would be looking for if I had a flashlight. Maybe some hair? Maybe that's what I want to see?

I don't know. I don't even know what I'm doing here. I don't even like her. I don't even like being with her. What am I doing here?

I sit up at the end of the bed and Ashley's got her eyes open and she's watching me. Shit, how long has she been awake?

"And what, pray tell, are you doing, my fine young friend?"

"Nothing. Just resting."

"Studying for your gynecological exam, Doctor?"

"What? No."

"Maybe it's time to take you home."

"Maybe."


My parents are so stupid. I don't know what's wrong with them. Ever since we moved here, they're always trying to get me to do things with them. They try to take me to the beach and to the park. My mom offered to take me to a movie. But it's just too weird.

My mom acts like everything is fine and we're all happy. Doesn't she realize that we never talk? We all hang out in different rooms and do different things. We all have about a twenty-foot radius of personal space around us. If I start walking toward the kitchen from the TV room and my mother is sitting at the kitchen table paying bills, she'll stand up and walk out onto the porch just so she doesn't have to interact with me.

And when my dad comes home from work and I hear the garage door open while I'm watching TV, I'll go upstairs and listen to music just so I don't have to be there when he walks in the door. We basically try to stay away from each other so we don't have to think about how my brother's not here.

It's not that he was such a great guy to have around. It's not like he was always the nicest or the coolest guy. But he was sort of the only one who ever talked at dinner. He was always talking about himself and about school and about which friends of his were being stupid.

And now it's like no one knows what to say. We're all just sitting around waiting for him to talk.

# EIGHT

**"O**h, honorable, admirable, and commendable Thespian, may I please have permission to speak?" Dan always says yes. He's the Thespian. I'm his plebe. It could be worse. He could be a real asshole about it. He could say no.

One embarrassing thing about being a plebe is having to beg every single Thespian before I can say anything to them. Oh, and I also have to be kneeling when I say it. Oh, and I also have to be wearing this fucking beanie.

The beanie is yellow and blue and my name is written on it in bubble paint. I have to wear it all day every day for the entire week. I'm supposed to wear it when I'm sleeping, but I don't, because who's going to check?

I don't know what the point is of all this stuff. When I signed up to become a plebe, I only did it because all of my friends are Thespians and I thought they would go easy on me, but it didn't turn out that way.

The first day was the worst so far. All the plebes had to gather outside the theater after school, and we had to figure out how to get into the theater before three o'clock. The only problem was, all the Thespians were in there holding the doors shut.

We tried the main doors and then ran down the hall to the side doors. We tried the stage doors and the outside doors, but they were all locked. A bunch of us started to panic, because if we didn't get into the theater we wouldn't be allowed to plebe.

Finally, one of the guys got through the side door, and we all pushed past the Thespians and into the theater. They were playing some Nine Inch Nails really loud through the sound system. I'm sure that was Dan's choice. He loves Nine Inch Nails almost as much as he loves Led Zeppelin.

As soon as we got in, someone grabbed my arm and made me sit down about halfway up the auditorium in a seat on the aisle. There weren't any other plebes around that I could see, so I was pretty much on my own at that point. I didn't know what the rules were going to be, but it didn't take me very long to find out.

A girl named Becky, who I've always liked and always thought of as a nice person, walked up to me and got in my face. She said, "What are you doing here, plebe? What do you want? You want to be a Thespian, plebe? Huh? Answer me!"

I started to answer, but as soon as I did, she cut me off. "Don't talk to me, plebe. Who do you think you are? You're just a plebe. You don't have permission to speak to me. I'm a Thespian."

I didn't know what to do at that point, because she was asking me questions and at the same time keeping me from answering. I thought it was kind of a stupid thing for her to be doing. I thought, It's not like Becky to be acting like the drill sergeant in *Full Metal Jacket*. It's not like her at all, so I raised my hand and lifted it toward her face, which was about three inches away from mine. Her breath smelled like hummus.

I lifted my hand, and I don't know why I did this, but I flicked her right in the middle of her forehead. Maybe I did it because she was too close, or because she was being such a bitch, but as soon as I did it, I wished that I hadn't. She screamed so loud that all the other Thespians could hear her. "A plebe just hit me in the face! A plebe just hit me in the face!"

As soon as she started screaming that, all the Thespians gathered around me and started yelling at me and humiliating me in so many ways that I can't really even remember.

All I know is that there was Marshmallow Fluff in my hair and there was lipstick smeared all over my face.

I was so mad when I saw my reflection. I was so mad at all those motherfuckers. I thought about quitting. I thought about walking away from the whole thing right then, because

I wasn't sure I could take a week of that shit from those motherfuckers, but then Dan called me on the phone and asked if I was okay.

He said, "You got it pretty bad today."

"Yeah," I said, because I was so mad I couldn't even say anything else.

He said, "Listen, that was the worst of it until the last night, okay? Don't quit. I won't let anyone do anything like that again. The first day is just supposed to scare people away, you know. You got through the first day, and now it's pretty much clear sailing until the last night. Don't quit."

He wasn't really asking me, he was more like telling me not to quit, so I didn't. I kept coming to school in that fucking beanie, and getting down on my knees every time I saw one of the Thespians and begging them to let me speak.

The worst was Phil, the long-haired hippy guy who's always talking about God and philosophy. But I don't know how you can think you're so smart when you smoke that much pot and flunk out of eleventh-grade English.

Every Thespian has a special greeting that they like to hear; some are quotes from their favorite movies, and some just like the standard "Oh, honorable, admirable, and commendable Thespian, may I please have permission to speak."

But Phil's is by far the longest. He likes for me to recite the last paragraph of Martin Luther King's *I Have a Dream* speech. He gave me a piece of paper with the speech written on it and asked me to memorize it.

It's not hard to memorize, because the words are so

simple and profound, but I don't think I understood how good a speech it was until I started saying it out loud.

But it was still embarrassing when I ran into Phil in the hallway between classes and started reciting the speech. *"When we let freedom ring, when we let it ring from every village and every hamlet, from every state and every city, we will be able to speed up that day when all of God's children, black men and white men, Jews and Gentiles, Protestants and Catholics, will be able to join hands and sing in the words of the old Negro spiritual, 'Free at last! Free at last! Thank God Almighty, we are free at last!' "*

I looked up after I finished the last sentence and saw Clarence, the security guard, standing with his arms folded, staring at me like he wanted to break my neck.

He motioned for me to come over to him with one finger, and I was scared that he was going to do something to me, like put me in a choke hold or something. I went over and he pointed at me with that same finger. I never realized fingers could have that many muscles before.

He put the finger in the middle of my chest, right where there's nothing but bone and skin, no muscles at all. It didn't really hurt, but it didn't feel too good either. It felt like he could have reached into my chest and pulled out my heart, like the guy in *Temple of Doom*, if he wanted to.

I was expecting him to say something, to let me know that he wasn't happy with what I'd just said in the hallway or to tell me not to quote Martin Luther King in front of him, but he didn't say anything at all. He just left that big finger in the center of my chest for a few seconds and then pulled it back and motioned for me to leave.

I didn't really know what to make of that.

Tonight is the last night of hell week. Induction. I've been hearing about this for so long, I'm kind of freaked out by it. Every plebe has to face their worst fears on induction night. I don't know how they know what your worst fears are, but I don't want to think about my worst fears. I want to be left alone.

I walk into the theater, ready for anything. I don't know what's going to happen, but I can tell it's something bad, because the theater is completely dark. Someone somewhere has a microphone and says over the sound system, "Sit down."

I sit in the first row of seats, because I can't see anything else. Who was that on the microphone? I couldn't tell.

Someone comes up behind me and ties something over my eyes. The cloth is soft, like a bandanna. I think it was a girl who tied the cloth around my eyes, because I could smell something like tropical fruit. Also, because of the way she tied the knot. She tied it tight, but not so tight that it hurt. If a guy had tied it, he would have tied it tighter.

Someone else kneels down in front of me and takes off my shoes. I hope my feet don't smell. I can't remember if these socks are clean.

Someone grabs me by the hand and makes me stand up. That's a girl's hand. She's pulling me somewhere. Where is she pulling me? Up onstage?

No, she's spinning me around in a circle. Shit, now I have no idea where I'm going. That has to be the idea. They must not want anyone to know where they're going.

They're pulling me again. They want me to follow them. They've got my right hand and they're pulling me toward something. I wonder what it is. I'm scared.

I've got my left hand out, feeling in the darkness. I don't want to run into anything.

My brother and I used to play a game like this. We saw an episode of *Magnum, P.I.*, where Magnum, T.C., and Rick were being held as prisoners of war in Vietnam. They were all blindfolded and being held in these bamboo cages. It was kind of disturbing, really, watching them get tortured and everything.

After that we went out in the backyard and played a game called POW. He put a blindfold on me, tied my hands behind my back, and led me around the backyard, like he was the Vietcong and I was a POW. He'd lead me in and out of the trees in circles, until I couldn't tell where we were, the whole time whispering this fake Vietnamese in my ear.

It got kind of scary, because after a while I started to believe that I was actually in Vietnam and that my brother wanted to kill me. When I was a kid, I could make myself believe anything.

They lead me into a room and force me to sit down on the floor. There are other people in here. They're grabbing my hands and feet. They're pulling me toward them. Who are these people? They're holding on to me so tightly.

I think they're other plebes. Their hands are sweaty, like they've been exercising.

I hear Dan's voice yelling in the background, "Hold on to each other. Don't let us pull you apart."

The other plebes hold on to me and I hold on to them. Someone grabs me by my shoulders and yanks me backward. The plebes hold on to me and pull me back into the circle. Someone to my left is being pulled out of the circle. Someone yells, "Grab her! Don't let her go!"

I reach out and hold on to something. I think it's an ankle, because it feels like I'm holding on to a sock. This is a girl's leg. I can tell because she's got short spiky hair on her legs, like she shaved her legs three days ago.

Someone else gets pulled out of the circle across the room, and people are screaming. This can't go on. This has got to stop. I hate this.

They've taken me out of the circle room and now I'm sitting in a chair. I think I'm in one of the dressing rooms, but I can't tell exactly. They're taking off my blindfold. Where am I?

God damn, that's a bright light. Shit, that's a spotlight. They're shining it right in my eyes from like three feet away. Ah, shit, I can't see anything. God damn it.

I close my eyes and turn my head. Someone says in an incredibly sarcastic voice, "What are you doing here, Brian?"

"What?"

"What are you doing here?"

"I . . . I don't know what you mean."

"What are you trying to prove?"

"I'm not trying to prove anything. I'm just—"

"Shut up. Don't talk back to me." I've heard about this. It's the Humiliation Room. They don't let you leave until you've humiliated yourself.

"Okay. Sorry."

"You think you're funny, don't you?"

"No. Well, kind of."

"You're not funny. You're not fucking funny. You're a piece of shit."

"Okay." I think whoever I'm talking to is a big fan of *Full Metal Jacket*. Oh, I bet that's Becky.

"Don't be sarcastic with me, you little fucking piece of shit."

"Sorry."

"Say it."

"Say what?"

"Say it."

"Oh, honorable, admirable, and—"

"Not that, you asshole. Say it."

"What do you want me to say?"

"Say it."

"What do you want me to say? I don't know what I'm supposed to say." This is turning into that scene from *Marathon Man*.

"Say it."

"It."

"No. Don't be a clown, you fucking piece of shit. Say it."

"But I don't know what you want me to say."

"You do know. You know, you piece of shit. You know."

"But I don't know. What?"

"Say it."

"What?"

"Say it."

"What?"

"Say it."

I don't know what they want me to say. Well, I've got an idea of what they want me to say. I've got an idea. The only thing is, I don't want to say it.

We sit in silence. My eyes have gotten used to the spotlight. I can see that there are three people standing behind the spotlight. I think they're all girls just by how tall they are.

I don't think they're going to let me out of here until I say it. It feels disgusting coming out of my mouth, like vomit, but I say it.

"I'm a piece of shit."

All the girls laugh when they hear me say it.

"All right, put his blindfold back on. He is a piece of shit."


I'm standing in front of a wall. I'm facing the wall. This must be the Fear Wall. Where you have to face your deepest fear. I can hear someone nearby crying. Jesus, I hope I don't cry, but it's been so long since I cried, maybe it would be good for me.

I wonder how they're going to know what my fear is. Everyone says that they have ways of finding out. I don't know how they're going to do that.

A guy comes up behind me and says, "Put your hands up on the wall."

I do. I feel like someone is going to put a gun to the base of my neck and blow my brains out.

The wall is tile. This must be the main hall, where we come into school. I reach up above my head and feel the ledge where the tiles end and the wood paneling begins.

The guy says, "Hold on." Who is that? I don't recognize that voice.

I wrap my fingernails on the edge of the tiles and try to hold on. There's maybe a quarter of an inch of space where the tiles end and the paneling begins, just enough to get a little bit of a grip.

If I were a rock climber and this was my only hold on a mountain, I would fall, which is why I'm not a rock climber.

The guy comes back over to me and whispers in my ear, "Get a good grip."

I hold on tighter. He grabs me by my shoulders and pulls down hard. My right fingers slip off the edge of the tile, but I hold on with my left and pull my whole body against the wall.

"Hold on," he says again. This time he sounds a little angry. He pulls me down again, harder this time.

Someone down the hall is screaming. What the hell is going on here? Is this really allowed inside a school?

The guy comes back behind me; he whispers, "What are you afraid of?"

That's it? That's how they find out what you're afraid of? They ask you? Well, that's not very scary. I say, "Cars," because that's what I'm most afraid of.

He says, "Cars?" like he can't really believe that's what I'm most afraid of.

"Crashes."

"Hold on to the wall." He pulls down on my shoulders and my left hand slips off. "Get up against the wall. Get flat up against the wall." I scramble to get my hand back up on the ledge.

I press my whole body against the wall. I try and make myself flat, like a piece of paper, against the wall.

I'm not really scared, but I do not like this feeling of being abused and controlled by other people.

"There's a car coming toward you, Brian. There's a car coming toward you. Get up against the wall. If you don't press up against the wall, the car is going to hit you. The car is going to hit you if you don't get up against the wall."

I press even flatter against the wall. I try and get my whole body against it. I don't want a car to hit me, even though I know that's not possible. It's not possible that there's a car coming, but I still have the feeling that there is.

It's like being in a dream where you're trying to run, but your legs move like they're in cold oatmeal. It's like that, but I'm awake and I can't get away from the car that's coming for me.

No way. I'm not going to cry. I'm not going to cry and

there's no way that these people here are going to make me think about that. I'm not going to think about that. There's no way.

They lead me back into the theater and put me in a seat. I can't tell what's happening. The blindfold is loosening and I can see just a sliver of light. I wonder if it's over. I can hear voices in the distance, but I can't hear what they're saying. The voices are getting closer.

Someone pulls me up and leads me by the hand up the stairs and onto the stage. I can see that some people are standing up here already. I can't tell if it's the other plebes or if it's the Thespians.

Someone unties my blindfold and takes it off. All the Thespians are standing around in a circle, smiling at me.

Dan is standing behind me. He was the one who took off my blindfold. He says, "Congratulations, Brian. You made it. You're a Thespian."

They all come over to me and hug me all at once. They're all saying, "Congratulations," and patting me on the back.

Wow, that was a lot to go through just to be able to eat in the theater.

# NINE

Monica and I have been dating for two weeks. Tonight is our two-week anniversary; she just told me she wants to have sex. I can't believe it. I can't believe how lucky I am to have found a girl like her, and I can't believe she wants to have sex with me.

We met during lunch period. I was just walking around talking to people, and I saw this kid I know from Latin—his name is Chris—and I went up to him and said, "What's up, Chris."

He said, "What's up," and then he introduced me to these two really cute girls who were sitting with him. Monica and Molly.

They're these really smart girls who take all the AP classes, and Monica is the head of the debate team. Molly is on the field hockey team.

Monica is the blond one. She has a really cute face and she's kind of hippyish. She only wears jeans and sweaters and she loves music from the sixties, which I think is the best music ever.

The other thing about her, which I love, is that she's so in touch with being a little kid. She loves *Sesame Street* and the Muppets. That is so cute. She's always talking about how different friends of hers are like different *Sesame Street* characters.

She says that I remind her of Gonzo—you know, the crazy space alien Muppet with the long blue nose that looks like a penis. Actually, the first time we ever got together she gave me a drawing of Gonzo that she did out of a coloring book.

It was so cute. It was a picture of Gonzo fishing, and she'd colored in the whole thing, and then she wrote her phone number in crayon and left it in my locker.

Monica says that she's Zoe. I'd never heard of Zoe before, but I guess she's kind of like Elmo but she doesn't get as much press.

Anyway, Monica is exactly like Zoe. They're both kind of hippyish and cute. The only difference is that one is covered in orange fur and the other is a puppet.

Ever since Monica and I started going out, everything in my life has been so much better. I just feel so close to her and so happy when I'm with her. It's probably disgusting, but I don't even care.

We talk on the phone every night and we see each other on the weekend for dates. The bad thing is when we have to be apart.

She went to Ohio for Thanksgiving with her family and I didn't see her for three days and it practically killed me. I just missed her so much. I missed everything about her. That's when I realized I was in love with her.

I wrote her a note and put it in her locker when we went back to school. Basically, the note just said how lucky I was to be with her and how happy I was that we found each other, and at the end I signed it *Love, Brian*.

That was the first time either of us had ever used the word *Love,* and ever since then we've been saying it to each other, about five hundred times a day.

We always call each other right before we go to bed and say we love each other. Everything is so perfect with us. I can't wait until we have sex. That is going to be awesome.

We've been making out ever since we first started going out. We've even taken our shirts off a few times, but we kept our pants on. I'd never been chest to chest with a girl before—kissing and making out and stuff.

God, that feels good. I never realized what that could feel like—having our chests pressed up against each other. It all feels so awesome. She's so warm and her skin is so soft.

She really likes it when I kiss her neck. She goes totally

crazy for that. She starts moaning and everything. So every time we make out I go straight for her neck, and pretty soon after that our shirts are on the floor. It's awesome.

Anyway, I guess a few times I've gotten a little carried away and left these major hickeys on her neck. Everyone at school was making fun of us for a while. And then, to get me back, she gave me a major hickey on my neck. She called it marking her territory. She even gave the hickey a name—she called it Lars, but I thought it looked more like Antarctica.

After I said that I loved her, we decided that we were going to have sex. Well, she decided, and she kind of told me. Well, she didn't tell me that we were going to have sex, but she told me that she'd gone on the pill, and I pretty much figured the rest of it out on my own.

So, tonight's the big night. I can't wait. I'm going to lose my virginity tonight.

It's going really good. I've got her pants off and it's only quarter past twelve. Her curfew is midnight, but I don't care. She's got her license, so it doesn't really matter. It's the most important night of my life. She can be a little late.

We're in my room, and because it's so far away from my parents' bedroom we can have music and everything. I've got Van Morrison playing. He's awesome. This is the perfect music to lose my virginity to.

The only thing is, I'm starting to get nervous. I'm trying to get my pants off, but I'm having trouble with the stupid zipper. It's not really going down. Damn. Okay, I got it.

I hope that didn't break the mood. Wow, I can't believe we're totally naked together. We've got all the lights off, so it's pretty dark, but the moon is out, so I can see a little bit.

What's going on here? As soon as I took my pants off I got really cold and my penis got soft.

Monica is shivering too. Did it just get incredibly cold in here? Usually, when we're making out, we get sweaty, but tonight it's different.

Also, for some reason our hips are about three feet apart from each other. I keep trying to get back on top of her, like I was before, but she won't let me.

I felt down there a second ago and I think I felt in the right place. I think she's ready. I just have to get on top of her and start doing it.

"Brian?" Wow, is she talking? That's not very romantic.

"Yeah?"

"I'm not sure if I'm ready."

"Okay. That's okay. Are you ready now?"

"No, I mean, I might not be ready at all tonight."

Jesus, I knew this would happen. "What? What do you mean?"

"I'm just . . . I might not be ready yet. Is that okay?"

"Um . . . what do you mean?"

"Well, I just started taking the pill a few days ago."

"So?"

"It doesn't really start working until you take it for a whole month. So is that okay?"

"Is what okay?"

"Are you mad?"

"No."

"What's wrong?"

"Nothing." I roll onto my side and face the other direction. This Van Morrison music is getting really annoying. I can't believe this.

Neither of us says anything for a while. I'm so pissed.

"Brian?"

"Yeah?"

"If you want . . . If you have a condom, we could try it that way."

I roll back over. "We could?"

I reach into the bedside table and pull out the pack of condoms I bought at the rest area in West Virginia last summer. I grab one out of the box and rip it open with my teeth. The little receptacle-tip thing is pointing up. I wonder if that means I'm supposed to put it on that way.

I put it onto my penis and start rolling it down, but there are at least two problems. One: Ever since she said that we weren't going to have sex, my penis has been in hibernation. And two: I think I have the condom upside down, so the whole thing is screwed up.

She says, "Do you know how to put one of those things on?"

"Yeah," I say. I've practiced before, but that was in the light. I don't think I'm doing it right. I flip it over so the latex rolls down the sides of my penis.

She's just staring at me with her legs crossed and her arms folded across her chest. She says, "I don't think you're supposed to flip it over once you've started putting it on."

What is she, like, the World Condom Expert now? If she knows so much, why isn't she helping? Lord knows I could use a little inspiration here.

Condoms smell gross.

I drop the first condom on the floor and get another one out of the package. There were three originally, but I used one to practice with when I got them. This is my last chance.

I tear open the wrapper and look at the thing in the moonlight. Okay, last time I had it receptacle up, and that was wrong, so I've got to make sure it's receptacle down so I can get it to roll right.

She's still just staring at me with her arms and legs crossed. Shit, I think I put it on the wrong way again. How the fuck did I manage to do that?

What's wrong with me? Shit, I've fucked this whole thing up.

I drop the second condom on the ground next to the first one and lie down next to her.

We lie next to each other. We're naked, but we're not touching. And we're staring up at the ceiling, and Van Morrison is still prattling on about dancing on the moon. What an ass.

Finally, she says the words that I've been waiting for. "Well, I should be getting home."

# TEN

I got my license. I'm free. I'm totally free. Now I can drive around and do whatever I want, and no one can stop me or anything. This is awesome.

It wasn't even that hard to get my license. I just had to take the class where you drive around with two other kids and get instructed by a guy in his thirties who's a total loser. My teacher had a ponytail—and you know that's the sign of a major loser.

The first time I drove, it was so stupid. They picked me up at my house in this little shitty-ass four-door car with a yellow triangle on top that said HAMPTON ROADS DRIVING SCHOOL—STUDENT DRIVER. God, that was so embarrassing. Why do they have to advertise it?

Anyway, I got in the back, because a girl was finishing her lesson, and after her it was my turn.

We changed drivers in a parking lot, and then Darrin—that was the instructor's name—told me we were going to go on the highway.

I adjusted my seat and checked the mirrors before I pulled out into traffic. I had to cross over four lanes before I could get into the left-turn lane to get on the highway. I got the left-turn-only green and pulled onto the on-ramp.

The car was a piece of shit, with no pickup at all, so I really had to stand on the gas to get it up to speed. Traffic moves pretty fast on the highway, and there were a lot of cars moving through the lanes.

Right about that time, as I was trying to merge into the next lane, I noticed this really terrible smell in the car. It smelled like something old and rotten. The first thing I thought of was that someone had farted, and I looked over at Darrin the loser and tried to tell by the way he was sitting if it was him. I couldn't tell, so I looked in the rearview mirror to see if I could tell if it was either of the kids in the back. Neither one of them was making a face or anything.

I hoped that no one thought it was me, because it wasn't, but the smell was getting worse, so I was about to say something when the brakes kicked in and the car slowed down all by itself.

At first I couldn't figure out what was happening, because I'd forgotten that Darrin had his own brake pedal.

I hoped he wasn't going to be sick or something. The smell in the car was so gross. It smelled like something had died and was rotting. I wondered if Darrin was a serial killer and had bodies stored in the trunk.

That's not that far-fetched, is it? Anyway, I looked up ahead and noticed that the traffic in front of us was completely jammed, and that's why Darrin had stopped the car.

We moved forward and the smell was getting stronger, and either something had died inside one of us or one of us was going to die very soon.

The guy in the backseat had pulled his shirt over his nose like a bandit. At least I wasn't the only one who smelled it.

The smell was seriously just about to kill me, when I noticed that there was a truck up ahead overturned on the side of the road.

It was a grocery-store truck, and it was flipped on its side and there were things all over the road in front of us, and that's what was causing the terrible smell.

I said, "What are those things?"

Darrin said, "Looks like chicken necks."

"What? Why chicken necks?"

"People around here use them to catch crabs. They hang them by strings off bridges and into streams."

Chicken necks on the asphalt, thawing in the afternoon sun, and I have to drive right through them.

I'm driving fast down Lynnhaven Road, away from school and away from home. Away from everything I can't stand anymore. Mom and Dad wanted me to help put up the

Christmas lights and the ornaments, but I can't do that. I just can't.

I've got the stereo on as loud as it can go. I love to drive. I thought it would be weird, but it's not.

I love my car. I love the way it turns and the way it handles the curves. There's so much power in that.

Fuck it. I'm just going to drive as fast as I can. Just fucking drive until the world flips upside down and I fall off.

I'm not dealing with this shit anymore. I can't live here anymore. I can't live anywhere. It's all too much. It's all too fucking much.

I take a right onto Shore Drive. It's the best road to drive when you feel like driving fast. It's two lanes. There are no streetlights—no traffic lights—and best of all, there's no place for cops to hide.

You can drive as fast as you want on Shore Drive and nothing can stop you—except maybe a tree.

A lot of people have died on this road. I see the sign saying how many—sixty-three since 1970. I don't give a fuck how many people have died on this road.

I put the pedal to the metal, and the car and I shoot down the road into the blackness. Nothing can stop me now, 'cause I don't care anymore.

I pass a cluster of little white crosses by the side of the road. Those look fresh. I bet those are the kids who died on this road last week. In the paper it said they were going at least ninety with five of them in the car. None of them were wearing seat belts, it was after school, and it was raining, and the paper said they didn't have their headlights on when they hit the tree.

That won't happen to me. I bet if I hit a tree I'd just bounce off and keep going.

I glance down at the speedometer—seventy. Shit, that's pretty fast. I wonder if I should slow down. I wonder if I should be more careful.

No, I wonder if I should turn my headlights off and just drive in the dark. Maybe I'll do that.

Shit, what was that? There was a light shining on me for a second. Where did that come from? I didn't see any other cars. What was that? It was like a white light from the sky and it shone on me from out of nowhere.

I'm slowing down. Okay, okay, I'm slowing down. Don't worry. I'm not going to crash my car. I'm not going to turn my headlights off.

What the hell was that light? All of a sudden there was this white light and I had this feeling like someone was watching me.

It was like something up in the sky opened up a spotlight on me for a second.

Wait. Maybe it was the moon. Yeah, it must have been the moon, because there wasn't anything else that could have shone that light on me, here in the middle of the darkest highway in the world.

The moon. It probably was just the moon shining through the trees.

# ELEVEN

I'm so sick of Monica. We've been dating for six weeks and we still haven't had sex. That is so annoying.

I'm so sick of her shit. She's been on the pill for a month, but she still says she's not ready.

I feel like I've been nice to her. I write her notes and call her every day. I don't get it. What do I have to do? This is getting absurd.

And another thing—what is up with her obsession with *Sesame Street*? I can't stand that anymore. I mean, we're not five years old here—there's no point in pretending that we are.

Another thing that annoys me is that she never shaves her legs. She's a feminist—okay, I get it, but what is that really about? I mean, she's so proud of her hairy legs; she's always pulling up her pant legs and showing them to me. It's kind of gross.

Her legs have more hair on them than mine do. I try to pretend that it doesn't bother me, but it sort of does. I mean, what is really so great about having legs that are hairier than a man's legs? Seriously.

Anyway, I have to figure out a way to break up with her, but I want to have sex first. Is that wrong?

# TWELVE

This week is the auditions for the new play. It's called *Children of a Lesser God*. I've heard of the movie, but I've never seen it. I guess it was a play first. It's about this guy who's a teacher at a school for the deaf, and he falls in love with this woman who is deaf, but she doesn't care about communicating with the rest of the world. It's pretty interesting, actually, because a lot of the play is in sign language, and everyone who gets a role in the play is going to have to learn how to do sign language.

I can't decide if I should try out for the play, because I'm not sure if I can do sign language.

I walk to the back of the theater where the sign-up sheet is and look at all the names on the list. Everyone on the list is a Thespian. I think I'm going to sign up. What the hell. Who's it going to hurt?

I take a pen out of my book bag and write my name as neatly as I can on the last blank line. As I'm writing, someone comes up behind me and pinches my butt. I turn around and Ms. Hanson is standing right there. She says, "I'm glad you're auditioning," and then winks at me.

Jesus, I can't believe Ms. Hanson just pinched my butt. I wonder if she is going to invite me over for a spaghetti dinner and seduce me.

During lunch I borrow the script from the library. I read the play all the way through, and the more I read, the more I can see the different characters and the way they might look and sound. The play is a little confusing to read, because the deaf woman, Sarah, signs something and then James, the main character, repeats it out loud. It's a really good play, though. The whole thing is supposed to take place in James's head while he's remembering all the things that happened between him and Sarah: how they met and how they fell in love and all the difficulty between them in their relationship.

Anyway, there are only a few parts and most of them are women, but there's one part I'm interested in. The character's name is Orin and he's a partially deaf student at the school. He's kind of funny too, because he likes to swear in sign language at hearing people who can't understand him.

I'm going to try out for this play and I'm going to get the part of Orin.

Auditions are after school at three. Everyone is nervous. People are walking around shaking their hands and mumbling to themselves. I'm nervous too. I'm not actually sure I can do this. I mean, I've never done anything like this before.

Ms. Hanson sits in the middle of the theater in the dark with a notebook and calls out people's names from the list. Dan goes up first, because he put his name down first, and stands on the middle of the stage. He starts a monologue from the beginning of the play. He's trying out for the lead role of James Leeds, the speech therapist.

He says, *"She went away from me. Or did I drive her away? I don't know. If I did, it was because . . . I seem to be having trouble stringing together a complete . . . I mean, a speech therapist shouldn't be having difficulty with the language. All right, start in the . . . Finish the sentence! Start in the beginning. In the beginning there was silence and out of that silence there could come only one thing: Speech. That's right. Human Speech. So, speak!"*

No one applauds when he's done, but I want to. He is such a good actor. Amy is next. I don't know a lot about her, I've just seen her hanging around the theater. She's pretty in a different way from most girls who are pretty. Instead of having one feature that looks really good, like her eyes or something, all her features look good together. Her face is soft—round eyes, a round nose, and cheeks that are a little bit chubby. She's auditioning for Sarah, the deaf girl. The play opens with a monologue by her, but it's all in sign lan-guage and no one knows sign language yet, so they're having the girls act out what Sarah's saying without words, to see if they can communicate to the audience.

What she's supposed to be signing is *"Me have nothing. Me deafy. Speech inept. Intelligence—tiny blockhead. English—blow away. Left one you. Depend—no. Think myself enough. Join, unjoined."*

I watch Amy closely to see if I can figure out what she's trying to say with her body. She keeps putting her hands over her head and shaking her head like she's trying to get sand out of her hair. I'm not sure that's exactly it, but at least she's trying. She's very passionate when she's up there.

A few other people go up, but I'm starting to get ner-vous, so I've stopped paying attention. Ms. Hanson calls my name and I go up onto the stage. I didn't realize how bright these lights are up here. Damn, it's hot and I can't see any-thing. I'm holding a page of the script that I'm supposed to read.

She says something to me, but somehow, because I can't see her, I can't hear her either. "What?"

"When you're ready."

"Okay." I'm out of breath. Why am I out of breath? I haven't even done anything yet. I look down at the words on the paper, but the light is so bright that it's hard to read them. I have to read the same speech Dan did, even though I know I can't do it as well as he did.

I want to get off the stage. I want to run out of here and

never come back. The words on the page are trembling. I re-member how it starts, though. I remember the first couple of sentences, so I put the paper down by my side and say, *"He went away from me."* I was supposed to say she, but I ac-cidentally said he. Shit. That's embarrassing. Maybe no one noticed. God, I hope everyone doesn't think I'm gay.

I look back down at my script just to make sure that I've got it right and then I keep talking. I feel more comfortable now that I've started. I kind of know how to pretend like what I'm saying is just occurring to me instead of already written down on the page.

I can feel the words sync up with my brain, and they feel like they're words that I want to say. *"In the beginning there was silence. . . ."* I pause, because I feel like there should be a pause there. If I were saying this, I would pause. I let the si-lence fill up the room for a moment, and I can feel people who weren't paying attention all of a sudden turn their heads and look at me.

*"And out of that silence there could come only one thing. . . ."* I think about it. I don't know what the one thing would be. But I understand the silence part. I pause again and take a deep breath.

There's adrenaline pumping through my body, but I feel completely calm. I say, *"Speech."*

I finish and walk off the stage, and people all throughout the audience are looking me right in the eye and smiling. Someone says, "That was great, man."

I sit down near Dan, but he doesn't say anything to me.

94

After auditions, we all go out to the coffee shop about a mile away. Dan drives me and Amy. I was going to ride shotgun, but then I realized that I should probably let the girl sit up front, so I pull the lever and the seat folds forward. I get in and Amy sits in front of me. I can smell her hair when she gets in the car. She has such nice-smelling hair.

Dan starts up the car and drives fast out of the parking lot. He says, "We're the best."

I'm not sure if he means me too, or if he's just talking to Amy. I lean back in the seat and look out the window. They're having a little romantic moment up there.

I glance at the two of them and I see Dan's hand slide over onto Amy's leg. Damn, I'd like to do that.

At the coffee shop, everyone from the theater is sitting around a table in the back. People are talking and telling stories. I sit on one side of Dan and Amy sits on the other side of him.

I wanted so badly to sit next to her. I don't know why, but I have this feeling like I want to be next to her. She's got a kind face.

Now she and Dan are holding hands under the table. That's not fair. I want that to be me.

I listen to the stories for a while. These people are pretty cool and pretty funny too. Sid tells a story about a time when he got so drunk that he accidentally went into the wrong house and slept in the wrong bed. Wow, that's really drunk. I try to think of a funny story that I can tell, because then Amy will pay attention to me.

Okay, there's a break in the stories. No one's talking. This is my chance. I say, "Hey, here's a scary story. This one time, you guys, I was sleeping, right? And it was probably, like, about three in the morning, you know. And I heard this sound, and the sound must have woken me up, because I woke up."

I like how everybody is watching me and paying attention, and even though I'm nervous, I still think it's a pretty good story, so I keep going. I glance over at Amy and she's still holding hands with Dan.

"And the sound was like—it sounded like a bear eating. It sounded like maybe a bear had come in from the woods and it was, like, feasting on a salmon or something? I didn't know what the sound was, but it was pretty gross-sounding, so I decided to go out into the hallway to check it out.

"I walked out into the hallway, and I could hear the sound clearer from there. It was definitely coming from inside the house."

Sid starts singing the theme from *The Twilight Zone*, which makes me laugh a little, but I keep talking.

"So I started walking down the hallway toward my parents' bedroom, because the sound seemed to be coming from in there. And the sound had changed. Now it sounded like an angry bear. It was grunting, and it was growling too.

"I kept getting closer, and I thought, Jesus, what am I going to do if I walk into my parents' bedroom and there's a bear in there? What if there's a bear in my parents' bedroom and it's eating them alive?

"I thought about going into the kitchen and getting a

knife, and I thought about getting a baseball bat from the basement. I didn't; I just opened the door slowly and looked into the bedroom.

"And what I saw was far more disturbing than any bear or anything I'd ever seen before. . . ."

I stop right there, pause for dramatic effect, and I can tell all the people are into the story and that they've all gotten sucked in by the details.

I push away from the table and get down on my hands and knees and twist my face into a pained expression. "What I saw was my father, on top of my mother, going like this. . . ."

I start humping the air and grunting like a big old bear. Everybody laughs, because they realize the point of the story is that I saw my parents humping. Which probably actually is the grossest thing I've ever seen in my life.

I look up at Amy and Dan after I'm done with my story, and they're kissing. Both of them have their eyes closed and Dan's lips are puckered and stuck way out. That's gross. That is really incredibly gross.

# THIRTEEN

**I** could literally pop right now. If someone stuck me with a pin, I probably would. I feel so happy and light-headed, like I've been sucking on helium balloons all day. This is awesome. This is the most awesome thing that's ever happened to me.

I'm going to be in the play. I'm going to play Orin. I can't believe it. This is it. I'm doing it. I'm going to act in a play.

I've never been in a play before. I'm going to have to learn sign language and act like I'm deaf, and I'm not sure if I can do it.

I mean, how am I supposed to figure out how to act like I'm deaf? There's so much about this whole thing that I don't know.

Oh well, I guess I'll just go in there and see what it's all about, and then if I can't do it, I'll just tell everyone that I'm sorry and that I can't do it. I hope that's okay.

First things first: We have to learn how to do sign language. Dan is playing James, the lead role, of course, and Amy is playing Sarah, the deaf girl.

Ms. Hanson has a friend who isn't deaf but knows sign language, and she's going to teach us. She takes us all into an empty classroom and starts teaching us the basics of American Sign Language. It's interesting, because I never realized this, but ASL—that's what you call it—is much different from how we speak.

Kathy, Ms. Hanson's friend, explains it. She says, "If you're using ASL and you want to say 'The cat is in the house,' you sign it like this." She makes a couple of signs and points to something. I don't really understand what she means, but she keeps explaining. "See, it's basically just 'There cat house.' And people understand what you mean, because the house can't be in the cat, right?"

We all laugh, because that's true. I like the idea of not having to talk, but people understanding me anyway. She keeps going. "In ASL you use your whole body, not just your hands. BE EMPHATIC!" She moves her arms and her whole body with such force it's kind of scary.

"If you're curious, be curious." She scrunches her face up and shrugs her shoulders. The way she moves is kind of cartoon-like. It's a little silly-looking, but I think she's just exaggerating for effect.

We learn the alphabet and a few basic signs, and then we

break up into groups to start learning our lines in sign language.

I try to get into Dan and Amy's group, but they are working together with Kathy. I get in a group with Cheryl, who's playing Lydia, this kind of slutty deaf girl who has a crush on Dan's character.

I'm a little worried about my friendship with Dan. Ever since I auditioned for the play, he's been acting weird toward me. The other day we were standing in the theater talking to everyone, and for some reason the subject of having a best friend came up and someone said to Dan, "You and Brian are best friends now, right?" I was going to say yes, but Dan just looked at me and said, "He's not my best friend."

I want him to like me. I want him to think I'm a good actor. I don't know why that's so important to me, but I really can't stand the idea that he hates me now for no reason. I really don't like that.

My brother used to get in these moods every once in a while. I mean, sometimes we'd be pretty close and we'd be hanging out and doing stuff together, and then, for no reason at all, he'd kind of shift and start acting differently. I don't know what that was about.

I always felt like it was my fault and that I'd done something wrong and that maybe if I acted in a different way then I could get him to come back around. But mostly the only thing that ever worked was just leaving him alone for a while—sometimes a few days—and then he'd start acting normal again.

I hated that about my brother. It was like everything in the house was under his control. If he was feeling something—if he was angry or upset—then everyone in the house would have to know about it.

He'd get so angry sometimes. It was scary. I remember one time at our old house, I was talking on the phone upstairs to one of my friends. I don't remember what I was saying. Oh, wait, yes I do. I was talking about him. I was talking about that he had tried out for the golf team at school and he was going to be a golfer. I don't remember if I was making fun of him or something—yeah, I guess I probably was. I was making fun of him, because golf is a stupid sport and I didn't understand why somebody like my brother would be trying out for the golf team.

Anyway, he must have heard me talking about him, because he came into my room without knocking, and I remember that I was lying facedown on my bed talking to my friend and he just started punching me in the hamstring. He didn't just punch me once. He punched me about fifteen times as hard as he could in the hamstring.

It hurt so much. I couldn't even scream. I just let out one sound—like an animal when its leg gets caught in a trap—and my friend on the phone asked me what had happened. I couldn't talk and I couldn't scream. I couldn't even stand up, because the pain in my leg was so bad. All I could do was put my face down into the pillows and cry.

I wonder if that was the last time I cried. I think it was. That was the last time I cried, and that was years ago.

Amy is running around the theater pretending she's a puppy. She's cute, the way she tilts her head and opens up her eyes really wide. She really does remind me of a puppy. She puts her hands up like they're paws and hangs her tongue out like she's panting and yelps a little.

She comes up to me with a piece of notebook paper that's rolled up and drops it in front of me. Does she want me to throw it for her? I pick it up and toss it a few rows back into the seats.

She scrambles over them, turning her head back and forth looking for the piece of paper. When she finds it, she brings it back to me and drops it in front of me again and then nudges my hand with her nose. I can't help but start laughing. It really is like she's a little puppy—playful and kind of annoying, but in a cute way.

I throw the piece of paper again and she brings it back to me. This time she curls up at my feet like she just got really tired and pretends to go to sleep right on top of my feet. I lean down and pet her hair like it's soft puppy fur.

God, I wish she wasn't dating Dan. I could fall for her so easily.

Ms. Hanson comes out of her office and starts up the rehearsal. She calls us all up onstage and we stand in a circle in the middle of the stage.

She says, "So, our first rehearsal is always a little tough. Before we do the read-through, let's do some exercises to get comfortable with ourselves and each other so we can begin to communicate. Only then can we create something that will speak to the audience."

She tells us all to sit on the stage, and we do, and then she calls out to Meredith in the back of the theater to cut all the lights. Ms. Hanson closes the curtain so that we're all completely in the dark. It's like being in a cave with a bunch of people I don't really know. This is so weird.

Ms. Hanson says, "Close your eyes." Her voice sounds like she's trying to hypnotize us, and I do feel a little like I'm being transported into another world.

She says, "Breathe," and we all take a deep breath. She says "Breathe" again, and again we all take the air into the bottom of our lungs.

No one says anything. We're all just relaxing, breathing together.

The theater is really warm, and with my eyes closed I feel like I'm about to go to sleep. I don't remember the last time I've been this relaxed.

Ms. Hanson whispers, "We are a family. We must rely on each other. We must trust each other. Who can you rely on? Who can you trust? You need something. What do you need?"

Everyone is completely quiet. This is so weird.

"With your eyes closed, go out and find someone."

Someone crawls right in front of me. Everyone else is moving, but I'm not. I'm sitting still.

I reach out and touch someone's hand. It's a girl's hand—I can tell because the skin is so soft. I wonder whose hand this is. Her hand is so soft and so warm.

She holds on to my hand and she doesn't let go. I wonder whose hand this is.

Ms. Hanson says, "This is the only person you can rely on right now. You need this person to survive. Open yourself. Give yourself. Take what you need from this person."

I'm still trying to figure out what she means by that when whoever is holding my hand lets go of it and grabs on to my face. I wonder what she's going to do. Is she going to squeeze my face or what? Oh no, she's pulling my face toward her.

Oh my God, she's kissing me. She's kissing me with her tongue and everything. Oh my God. This is awesome. I'm trying to think of what I need from her, but all I can think about is that I'm being kissed by a girl and her lips are so unbelievably soft.

There's so much softness in the world right now, and it's so warm. Oh my God, this is great.

I'm kissing her too. I hope I'm doing a good job. I hope I'm using my tongue in the right way. She swirls her tongue around my tongue and there's a chill running up my spine, and I think I've forgotten how to breathe.

She tastes like spearmint, and her kisses are so warm and delicious. I don't think I've ever been this happy.

Ms. Hanson says something that I don't hear, and the girl lets go of my face and pulls her lips away from mine. I hear people scrambling around in the dark. Who was that? Who kissed me? Who was that? I think I'm in love.

Someone turns the lights back on and we all squint and wait for our eyes to adjust. I look around at the girls' faces to see who it was that kissed me. Who was that?

No one is looking at me. One of them should be looking

at me. The one who kissed me should be looking at me and smiling, right? Cheryl?

No one is looking at me. I hope it was Amy.

Dan drives Amy home and I sit in the back.

I can't help but look at Amy's face—actually, the side of her face. I think I might be falling in love with her. She's got such smooth skin and nice hair. God, she has nice hair. When she was pretending that she was a puppy and she came up to me and made me pet her, that might have been when I started to fall in love with her.

I can't fall in love with her, though. I can't. She's Dan's girlfriend, and Dan is the man.

I don't even want to have sex with her, that's how much I like her. I just want to sit in a room with her and figure her out. I want to lie on my roof and look up at the stars and hold her, and then I want to whisper in her ear that I'm in love with her and that she's the girl for me and that she should get rid of Dan. But I can't do any of that.

# FOURTEEN

Dan and Amy and I are getting drunk. I've had drinks before, but I've never really been drunk. This is awesome. This is an awesome feeling. I've had a couple of drinks—orange juice and gin, just like the rappers drink—and I'm already feeling it. I'm feeling kind of numb in my head and tingly in my hands.

"Oh my God, you guys are awesome." I don't know why I just said that. Why did I say that?

This is so cool. My parents are out late—so we're up in my room drinking, which is awesome.

"You guys are awesome." Why did I say that again?

Dan is the bartender. He's mixing the drinks, and Amy

and I are drinking. Dan's not drinking because he has to drive Amy home later.

I put on the stereo. You know what I want to listen to? You know what I want to listen to? I want to listen to some eighties music.

Awesome. Awesome. I find my favorite song from when I was a kid. Oh my God, this is awesome.

They're going to love this. "You guys are gonna love this."

The opening drum part kicks. Oh my God, that's awesome. I can't help it, I'm dancing. Yes. The guitar is awesome. That's so eighties. I'm dancing. "You guys, check it out."

*Now I gotta cut loose, footloose*
*Kick off your Sunday shoes*

Jesus, I'm out of breath. That was so awesome. "You guys, that was awesome." I was dancing like such a freak. I was dancing like Kevin Bacon. "You guys, that was awesome. Wasn't that awesome, you guys?"

I sit down on my bed. Dan and Amy aren't paying attention to me. They're making out on my bed. They're always doing that. They're always making out and never paying attention to me.

That's depressing. Why do they have to make out on my bed? Can't they make out in his car or something? Whatever.

Oh, I just remembered I've got this movie camera in my

drawer. I'm going to make a movie of them making out. I open up my drawer with the old birthday cards and the honorable-mention ribbon from the fourth-grade science fair and grab the old eight-millimeter camera.

It doesn't work, but I think it will be funny to pretend like I'm a movie director and I'm shooting a porno or something.

Ha-ha. They're making out. That's hilarious. They're hilarious.

I love this. This is, like, the best night of my life.

I'm bored. What am I going to do, just sit here and watch them make out? Whatever.

I lie down on the floor and look up at the ceiling fan. That's awesome. I can't believe how awesome that is. The ceiling fan is, like, the best. It reminds me of *Raiders of the Lost Ark*. That was an awesome movie.

"You guys." They're not answering. "You guys, remember when the monkey ate the date in *Raiders of the Lost Ark?* Wasn't that sad, you guys? Remember when the monkey died—wasn't that sad?"

I need to drink more often. Drinking makes you think of such awesome stuff. There's so much awesome stuff to think about when you're drinking, and drinking makes it all so much better to think about.

I'm bored.

I just need to think more. That's what I need to do. That's what people don't understand about me. People don't understand me because, a lot of the time, I'm thinking they won't understand me, but actually, if I was just not that worried about it, I could get them to understand me better than what I'm doing now.

You know what would be awesome? If we were on a boat and it was, like, sunset and there was all this stuff around, and the sky was . . . Oh, never mind. I think I drank too much. I think the room is spinning. Is the room spinning?

I think the ceiling fan is making me kind of sick. Yeah, it's making me dizzy. The ceiling fan sucks. Why is it even on? I hate the ceiling fan.

This is a bad feeling. The room spinning is a bad feeling.

Dan and Amy are standing up. What are they doing? Amy comes over to me; she's so nice. God, I wish she was my girlfriend. "Hey, you okay?"

She's drunk too. That's awesome. I'm glad somebody's drinking with me.

"I'm okay," I say.

"You wanna come?"

"What! Where?"

"I just asked you."

"No you didn't. You didn't ask me anything."

"Yes I did. I asked you if you want to come to 7-Eleven with us."

"Oh, why are you going to 7-Eleven?"

Dan says, "We're going to buy some candy." He's not drunk at all. That's lame.

"What kind of candy?"

"Lubricated."

They got back from 7-Eleven like a half hour ago, and Dan and Amy are in my bathroom together. What are they doing? They've been in there forever. Jesus, this sucks.

I wonder when my parents are getting home. I bet they're getting home soon. They're probably going to be asking me a bunch of questions, but that's okay. I'm a good actor. I can pretend like I'm sober in front of my parents.

Finally, Dan and Amy come out of the bathroom. I wonder what they were doing in there? Seriously, what were they doing?

I wonder if they had sex in there. I hope they didn't have sex in my bathroom while I was just sitting here hanging out.

Oh shit, my parents are home. My parents are home. Fuck, what am I going to do?

"Hide the gin, you guys, put the booze away. Put the booze away, you guys."

Dan picks up the booze and takes it into the bathroom. Amy and I sit next to each other on the bed. We're good actors. We'll be fine.

Someone's knocking on the door. Shit, okay. Get ready for the greatest performance of my career.

"Come in." Mom opens the door. Amy and I are just sitting here not doing anything; nothing is going on.

"What's going on in here?"

"Nothing. How was your show?" I think they went to a play. I can't remember what it was called.

"It was fine. Hi, Amy, how are you?"

"I'm fine, how are you?"

"I'm fine. How is your school year going?"

"It's going well. I'm learning slow much." Amy just slurred her words. I hope Mom didn't notice.

"Good. Good. How's the play going?"

"It's going great. It's the shingle greatest experience of my entire life." Shit, she slurred her words again.

"Good. Good. Well, you guys be good."

"We will."

She closes the door. I wonder if she knew. I wonder if it smells in here. Does it smell? The fan has been on for the entire night, so it probably doesn't smell that much.

Shit. Dan comes out of the bathroom. He was hiding in there. He's laughing to himself.

"Why are you laughing?"

"You're a couple of fucking drunks."

"Do you think she knew?"

He laughs. "The shingle greatest experience of my entire life."


Dan and Amy left an hour ago and I've been lying in bed trying to go to sleep. Oh God, I feel sick. What was I thinking? What was I . . . Oh God.

Every time I close my eyes, it feels like I'm on a Tilt-A-Whirl. Ugh. Oh God. I hope I don't throw up.

I can't close my eyes, because then I feel like I'm going to throw up. There's so much gin and orange juice down in my stomach, it feels like the ocean down there. Except instead of water it's orange juice and gin.

When did this stop being fun? How much did I drink?

Oh God. A little just came up into my mouth. That's gross. Oh God. Ugh. I'd better go to the bathroom.

Oh God. I don't know if I'm going to make it to the toilet.

Oh God. Why did I start drinking? Why? Why?

Why didn't anyone tell me it was going to be like this? Oh, this isn't fun. This isn't fun at all.

# fIfTEEN

We're working so hard on this play. It's exhausting. I mean, we just have so much to do. It's not only learning our lines and where to stand on the stage and everything, but we also have to learn this whole new language.

Ms. Hanson says that near the end of rehearsals we're going to go into Norfolk and have this silent retreat, where we can only speak in sign for a whole day, and then spend a night at a hotel. I can't wait for that.

After rehearsal, Dan and I drive Amy home, and I watch from the car as they make out on the porch for about twenty-five minutes. Finally, Dan gets back in the car and we drive away. He turns the stereo up loud, so I can't ask him what I want to ask him, which is, Are you guys in love?

Amy lives pretty far away from where Dan and I live, and we have to get on the highway to get home. He's doing his thing again with the songs on the radio. The Dan Effect, that's what I'll call it.

We pull up to the toll station—it's a quarter every time you come through here. Dan slows down in front of the coin basket and pulls a penny out of the ashtray thing. He's got a couple of quarters in there too. I wonder why he didn't take one of those?

He throws the penny into the basket and the red light that is supposed to turn green stays red. Dan pulls through the toll stop anyway. The alarm bell goes off. What the hell is he doing? He's going to get pulled over.

I yell over the music, "Why did you do that?"

He turns it down and says, "They can't tell if I threw in a quarter or a penny, so why would I waste twenty-four cents?"

I guess I see his point, but I wouldn't do that. Dan is the kind of guy who's always looking for ways to make his life easier.

We're supposed to get off at Exit 27, but instead we get off at Exit 25.

"Where are we going?"

"You'll see."

We cross Virginia Beach Boulevard and turn in to a residential area. These are mostly condos and little row houses.

It's not as nice a neighborhood as where Dan and I live, but it's not a terrible neighborhood either.

We park in front of a brick condo, get out of the car, and walk up to the door. I still don't know whose house this is or what the hell we're doing here. I think Dan likes to keep secrets.

He rings the doorbell and, after a minute, Cheryl opens the door. She doesn't seem surprised to see us, she just says, "Oh, hey, guys. Come on in."

Her house smells like cat pee and stale cigarette smoke. She leads us into the kitchen and we sit at the table. Nobody is really saying anything.

A little black cat jumps from the kitchen counter onto Cheryl's lap. She holds it up to her chest and introduces us to it. "Midnight, this is Dan and Brian. Say hello." She grabs the kitten's paw and waves it at us.

Dan says, "Cute." He reaches over and strokes its ear with one finger.

I stand up and pet its little head. I'm more used to petting dogs, so I accidentally pet too much of its head and the back of my hand rubs against Cheryl's breast. Oops, I didn't mean to do that, but that felt good, so I do it again, and the second time I make sure to let my hand rub against her breast a little more.

I don't want to push my luck, so I stop and sit back down. I just realized what we're doing here. Dan is trying to set me up with Cheryl. That is so awesome. He is such an awesome friend. He brought me over here so I can dump

Monica, go out with Cheryl, and have sex and lose my virginity.

I'm so happy. I look at Dan and smile. I shouldn't have been thinking all that bad stuff about him, just because other people told me things. That really wasn't cool. I feel like an asshole.

I want to think of something really cool to say to Cheryl. What should I say? Maybe I'll do my Sean Connery impression and say, Cheryl, you've got a cute kitten, but I want to see your pussy.

That probably wouldn't work. I'm such an asshole. I hate myself. Maybe I should say, I've got a pool at my house, you could come over and swim sometime. Hey, if girls come over to my house to swim, maybe I could figure out a way to see them naked. That would be the best.

While I've been thinking, Dan and Cheryl have been staring at each other. I wonder what he's doing. Why is he staring at my new girlfriend like that? Well, she's not my girlfriend yet. I just have to figure out what to say to her and then we'll fall in love and have sex. So why is Dan staring at her, and why is she staring at him?

I keep looking at both of them, waiting for them to notice that I'm here in the room with them, but they're not noticing. I clear my throat, hoping that's going to get their attention. It doesn't.

After another minute Dan says, "Where's your bathroom?"

Cheryl says, "I'll show you."

They both go down the hall together, out of sight. She

should be back in just a few seconds and by then I'll have figured out what I'm going to say to her to make her fall in love with me. But she's not coming back and neither is he.

The whole house is disturbingly quiet. I should be able to hear someone going to the bathroom, or a toilet flushing, or a sink running. I'd like to hear something—maybe a conversation, or an argument, but I don't hear anything.

Wait, I think I just heard someone moan. That's not good. That was not the sound I wanted to hear at this moment.

Okay, I'll just sit here and wait for them to come back. I'm sure they won't be long. I'm sure they're just having a little intimate moment and then they'll be done and they'll come back.

But they're not coming back and I think I just heard another moan. That sounded like her moaning. Gross.

What the hell am I doing here? I should get up and go out to the car, or start walking home or something. I think we're only about five miles from my house.

I should get up, but I don't. I just sit at the kitchen table and look at the cat's water and food bowls. Midnight comes back into the kitchen and jumps up onto the countertop.

She tilts her head and looks at me, and I can tell what she's thinking. She's thinking, What the fuck are you doing here?

Dan comes back to the kitchen after about twenty minutes. Cheryl doesn't. He just taps me on the shoulder and we go back out to the car. I think about calling out good-bye to

Cheryl, but I don't, because I'm not sure I ever want to talk to her again.

Once we get out to the car, Dan puts the key in but doesn't start it. He looks at me with as serious a face as a person can have and says, "Don't tell Amy."

He drives me the rest of the way home and we don't say anything to each other.

I wish my brother was here. I wish we were playing Nerf football in the backyard. He would be the quarterback and I would be the receiver and I'd run the perfect patterns.

I'd run the buttonhook and the post. I'd run the deep-outs and the slants. He'd always throw the perfect spiral. He'd put it right on my shoulder and if I could touch it, I would catch it. I wish he was throwing me a spiral right now.

In our backyard, before we moved, we had this whole little field set up. I'd run up the little hill we had back there and cut to the right, shaking off the coverage, and then cut back to the left, toward the fence post.

I'd dive with my eyes on the ball and it would land right there in my hands. I'd always dive even if I didn't need to. He'd put it right there and I would dive for it.

# SIXTEEN

I've got a date with Monica tonight. It's our three-month anniversary. God damn it, I've been going out with her for a long time. I can't believe we haven't had sex yet. What's wrong with her? What's wrong with me?

We're going to one of those old movie theaters with the big marquee outside and the flashing lights. They even have a balcony. It's great. We're going to see a double feature of Chinese cinema, so I figured we should try out the Chinese restaurant on the corner. Is that romantic? I don't know.

My dad gave me some money so I could pay for dinner. That was cool of him. He handed me a couple of twenties and said, "Don't tell your mother," even though she was standing right there. He's funny when he wants to be, I guess.

We order some spring rolls and Monica starts up with a conversation about her last therapy session. "Oh, Susan said we're leaving the honeymoon behind."

"What?" Susan is Monica's new therapist, and Monica is forever quoting Susan to me. I really hate that. Monica lives by what Susan says, though. She takes whatever Susan says as gospel, and for some reason that annoys the shit out of me.

"She said we're leaving the honeymoon portion of our relationship behind. She said that we're dealing with the real stuff now."

Is it weird that she thinks the honeymoon portion of our relationship lasted three months? I thought it was like two weeks. I raise my eyebrows and try to look interested.

"Susan says there are two commandments I should live by. One: Love thyself before all others. Two: Thou shalt not bullshit thyself."

Oh my God, if I have to hear one more thing about Susan I'm going to choke on this spring roll. I try to be nice about it. I say, "Do you really need commandments to live by?"

"No, but it's so true. It's . . ." She touches her fingers to her lips and kisses them, like an Italian would do, as if to say,

Susan's words are perfect. That's another thing that annoys me about Monica. Sometimes she pretends she doesn't speak English and that she doesn't have the vocabulary to describe what she's thinking, so she uses European hand gestures to make her point.

I say, "Do you really think those words are perfect? You think those words are good words to live by?"

"Absolutely." She kisses her hand again. What the fuck is that?

"You don't think . . . I mean, don't you think it's kind of stupid to live your life based on someone else's commandments?"

She leans back from the table. Oops, I think I said too much. She says, "Okay."

"What?"

"Nothing."

"What? What did I say?"

"You know what you said."

"No. What did I say? Did I hurt your feelings?"

She laughs, but not in a happy way, in the way a girl laughs when her boyfriend hurts her feelings on their three-month anniversary at a Chinese restaurant.

We sit in silence, chewing on our spring rolls.

The waitress comes with our entrées and we eat with our faces tipped toward our plates.

I look up at her with my head tilted down, like Malcolm McDowell at the beginning of A Clockwork Orange, when he's getting drugged up at the Korova milkbar and the camera pulls back from the extreme close-up all the way out to a long shot.

She says, "What?"

"What?"

"Why are you staring at me?"

"Because I hurt your feelings, and I didn't mean to."

"You did hurt my feelings."

"How?"

"You called me stupid. I'm not stupid."

"I know. I know you're not. I didn't mean that. You're not stupid." Her face softens a little. She's getting over it. "How's your dinner?"

"It's so good. How's yours?"

"Good." She's an easy person to make up with. I just have to change the subject and we're fine. "I'm so excited about these movies."

"Me too, especially the Ang Lee one."

"Yeah, that one is supposed to be great." Before she met me, she'd never heard of Ang Lee; now she's like the Ang Lee expert of the world.

I wonder if we'll have sex tonight when we go back to my house. I can't believe we haven't done it yet. This is absurd.

The check comes and I pay it with the twenties my dad gave me.

We get up and leave the restaurant together. I go ahead and open the door for her. I think it's nice to treat a lady like a lady. Also, maybe it will get me laid.

Monica says, "Susan says opening doors is part of the honeymoon phase. You don't have to do that anymore; we're not in the honeymoon phase anymore."

Tell me about it.

# SEVENTEEN

**D**an's here with a couple of girls from school. They're younger than us. They're freshmen. Tessa and Vicky. Tessa is the blonde. Vicky is the brunette. They're both pretty cute.

Dan says he's going to take Tessa. I can have Vicky. I don't know—cheating on my girlfriend? I don't know if I can really do that. It just seems wrong.

Tessa has been drinking something—rum, I think. She got it out of her dad's liquor cabinet.

We're back over at my house now. Hanging out in my room, because my parents apparently don't care if we get drunk up here, but I'm not in the mood to get that drunk.

Tessa and Vicky are dancing around my room singing a

song they learned in elementary school. I think it's the school theme song, but I'm not sure.

Freshmen girls have a lot of energy.

Dan and I are just watching them dance around. They're kind of sexy in an innocent way.

They finish their song and Tessa comes over and sits on Dan's lap. God, she's all over him. What a slut.

Vicky sits next to me on the floor and we start talking about music. I don't think she's as drunk as Tessa. She is kind of cute, though. I wonder if I should make a move.

Tessa stands up, holds Dan's hand, and leads him into the bathroom. God, he gets a lot of action in there.

Vicky says, "Tessa, what are you doing?"

"Nothing."

"Tess, you okay?"

"Yes, Mother."

Vicky looks at me and says, "She's going to get herself in trouble."

"What do you mean?"

"She really likes him."

"Oh."

"He's got a girlfriend, though, right?"

"Yeah. Amy."

"Ugh. She's such a bitch. I hate her."

"Really?" How could anyone hate Amy?

"Tessa thinks if she hooks up with Dan he'll dump Amy."

"Yeah . . . Well, we'll see, I guess."

Vicky doesn't say anything. She just stands up and turns on the radio. It's after midnight. I never listen to the radio after midnight. She tunes it to the Coast and picks up the phone and starts dialing a number.

I wonder who she's calling? Who could she possibly be calling after midnight?

She says, "Is that Stevie?" Who the fuck is Stevie? Some other guy? "Yeah, hey, it's Vicky. What's up?"

Is she seriously calling some other guy from my room while her best friend is hooking up with my friend in my bathroom?

She's still talking. "No—I'm at some guy's house." She laughs really long, like the guy on the phone said something really funny. She says, "No—he's definitely not my boyfriend."

This is just obnoxious. I guess that's what you get for inviting freshman girls over to your house.

I can't help myself. I say, "Who are you talking to?"

She looks at me like she can't believe I interrupted and says, "Little Stevie from the Coast."

"You mean the DJ?"

"Yeah." Right, of course. You're calling a DJ in the middle of the night while your best friend is hooking up in my bathroom. Right, of course you are. Stupid of me to not understand that. Of course you're calling a DJ. Actually, could you get off the phone? Because I need to call Wolfman Jack.

If I said that, she probably wouldn't even understand what I was talking about. She probably hasn't even seen *American Graffiti*.

She's still talking to Little Stevie. "What? No—I'm not going to hook up with him. Are you crazy? No—he's just some guy I'm hanging out with until my best friend gets out of the bathroom."

I noticed that she didn't mention her best friend is hooking up in the bathroom. People only say what they want you to know.

I go over and sit on my bed and pick up a book from the bedside table. If nothing's going to happen, I might as well get some reading done.

She looks at me again from across the room and says, "Ugh, I don't know. No, he's not very good-looking."

Jesus, when did this become my life?

Finally, Dan comes out of the bathroom. He looks happy. He says, "Vicky, you ready? I'm going to give you a ride home."

Tessa comes out of the bathroom a second later. Okay. I guess I know what went on in there.

# EIGHTEEN

I'm making my way through the hallways toward my fourth-period Algebra II class. Algebra is so boring.

There are a couple of really cute girls standing at their lockers on the left side of the hallway. I kind of want to go over there and rub up against them, like I used to at the beginning of the year. That was fun.

They have such short skirts on and they're wearing these tight tank tops that show their midriffs. God, it would be so easy just to go over there and rub up against them. It would be so easy.

I move toward them, but then I see Nat, that guy from the bus who has something wrong with him. He's wearing his winter coat with the fur hood even though the weather is pretty warm. He's moving toward the hot girls too. God, I wonder if he's going to rub up against them.

I think he is. I can tell because he uses the same technique I do. He puts his hand down at his waist and makes it dead. He's getting closer to the girls. I think he's going to do it.

He rubs the back of his hand along one girl's butt, but the hallway isn't really crowded enough to pretend like it was a mistake, and she turns around and yells at him, "Get your fucking hands off me, you fucking pervert!"

Jesus, I'm glad that wasn't me. What the fuck? She just totally flipped out at him in the middle of the hallway. His face is getting red and he's walking away fast.

She's not letting it go. "Hey, come back here, you pervert! Come back here!"

The girl is about to chase Nat down the hallway, but she sees me watching and says, "Did you see that? Did you see what happened?"

"Yeah, I saw." I don't know why I said that.

"Do you know him? Do you know that guy?"

"Uh, yeah, a little . . . He used to ride my bus."

"And you saw what happened?"

"Yeah, he, uh, he groped you in the hallway."

"Yes. Thank you. Finally, someone saw." Boy, I guess this has happened before. "Will you testify?"

"Testify?"

"Will you talk to the principal about it, if they call you down to the office?"

"Uh . . ." Well, maybe I'm not the best person to talk to about rubbing up against girls in the hallway.

"Please."

"Okay." Fuck, why did I just agree to testify against another hallway molester? That's like John Wilkes Booth testifying against Lee Harvey Oswald—well, it's not exactly like that.

She writes my name down on a piece of paper and goes straight to the office with it.

I'm not exactly sure what bad karma is, but I think this may be it.

# NINETEEN

God, I've got to get to sleep, but I can't slow my mind down. I want to stop thinking, but I can't. I can't think and I can't stop thinking.

I've got to learn my lines. I don't know my lines at all. I don't even know how to act like I'm deaf. I'm going to get up there and start stuttering and spitting on myself. Maybe I should just . . .

What did it feel like to be driving that fast? What did it feel like when the car went off the road? Did it feel like flying or was it like a roller coaster going off the tracks? Did the steering wheel hit him? Did the glass? Did his face get cut by the glass? Could he see? Could he breathe? Could he yell?

Why didn't anyone hear him? Why didn't anyone see

him in the ditch? They could have driven by and seen him in the ditch and called 911. Why didn't they hear the car crash? Did they do CPR?

Did he float above it all? Was he watching it all happen from above? Did he know he wasn't going to make it? Was he trying to die? Did he want to die?

I get out of bed and pace around the room. I've got to figure out how to act deaf. I don't know what that would be like. Not just not being able to hear, but how do you feel different? Do you feel different?

My ears would feel numb, like their only job was to hold up sunglasses. Things would be quiet all the time—so quiet that my brain wouldn't even know what sound was like. Sound would just be vibration. I'd only feel sound, never hear it.

See, but it's not just about that. It's about the way it would feel to talk. I couldn't hear myself. I couldn't hear any of the things that were coming out of my mouth. My first line, I'm supposed to be doing this speech exercise with a bunch of S's in it.

It goes, *"Speech is not a specious but a sacred sanction, secured by solemn sacrifice."*

I close my eyes and try and close my ears too. I tell my brain to shut off my ears. How does it feel to say something you can't hear?

"Speech. Speech." The S is a hard letter to say if you can't hear it. My tongue is right behind my teeth and I'm trying to make the sound without hearing it. The difference between the S sound and the TH sound is really small.

There's hardly any difference at all. It's just where the tongue is behind the teeth.

My S's sound like TH's when I don't have my tongue in the right place. *"Thpeech ith not a thpeciouth but a thacred thanction."*

That's not right. I sound like I'm trying to be retarded. I put my head under my pillows and try again. One of the things that's so hard about the S is that I can't feel it when I say it. I can feel the Z sound because it's more in the back of the throat and it vibrates. Maybe I can learn to make my S sound by practicing my Z sound.

"Zzzzzzz. Sssssss. Zzzzzz. Ssssss." I sound like a snoring snake.

Forget about sound. Let all the sound disappear. Do it by feel, not by sound. By feel.

*"Speechs ith not a thepisous but a sacred sanctiona."*

I'm getting it. I'm getting there. Maybe I can teach myself how to talk.

# TWENTY

I can smell breakfast all the way up in my room. Waffles. That's one thing about my parents—they might not be the best cooks in the world, but they make a pretty good breakfast every once in a while.

I go downstairs, sit down at the breakfast table across from Dad, and Mom puts a plate in front of me. No one says anything to me. Mom half-smiles at me, but I can't smile back.

Waffles are my favorite, because I like to prepare them a special way. I spread the butter evenly across all the pockets and let it melt in there, and then I cut up the waffles into seventy-two equal pieces—one square per piece. Then I pour the syrup over all the pieces, so each one can soak up more syrup per piece. Also, I only use pure Vermont maple syrup, not that Mrs. Butterworth's shit that my mother uses.

My brother always used to get mad at me because I used so much syrup. He'd say things like, "Don't you know how much that stuff costs?"

He was probably right. It probably does cost a lot, but it wasn't like he was paying for it. My brother had a real temper problem. He'd get mad at me for the stupidest shit. I don't know why. He'd just get so angry all the time, for no reason. Like if I went into his room without asking and he found out, he'd hold me down and punch me as hard as he could until I started crying. During dinner, he was always talking about who he was pissed off at.

I finish my waffles and look over at my parents. They're all dressed up. I say, "Are you going somewhere?"

My dad looks surprised, either because he didn't know I was there or he didn't know I knew how to talk. He says, "We're going to see your brother."

Oh, I should have known that. Has it been a year? A whole year? I guess it was a year ago. God.

All of a sudden I feel like going back into my room and locking the door.

My mother sits down next to me and leans forward. "Do you want to come with us?" She's nodding her head while she's saying that, hoping, obviously, that I'm going to say yes.

I look at her and go back upstairs and lock the door to my room. You know who I hate? God. I hate God. Not that

I even believe in him or anything, but if he does exist, then I hate him so much, I can't even stand how much I hate him.

I sit at my desk and look out the window at the pool and the boathouse and the swampy river. The tide is out and the water has turned into thick, sloppy mud. I watch a crane fly-ing low over the mud and the cattails. It lands in the swamp and stands on one leg.

If God doesn't exist, then how could there be something so beautiful in the world? I don't know. Maybe he does exist, but he just didn't care about my brother. Or me. That's prob-ably it.

I open the drawer to my desk. I've got the most random shit in here. I've got a birthday invitation from when I was six and three dice from Yahtzee. A business card that my dad had made up for me at work, with my name and our old phone number. I've got a whole bunch of pencils from when my friends and I used to pencil fight in school. That sign my brother made in Shop class. And a Ping-Pong ball.

I take the Ping-Pong ball out and put it on the desk. It sits still because the surface is even, but if I rest my hand near the ball it rolls a little bit. If God exists, then he should move this Ping-Pong ball without me doing anything.

"I'll make a deal with you," I say to God. "If you move this Ping-Pong ball, I'll believe in you, okay? Really, you don't have to move it a lot. You don't even have to make it float or anything. I'm not asking for a miracle. I'm just ask-ing for you to move it a little. Move it a little and I'll believe in you."

I wait for him to move it, just a little, but nothing is happening yet. Maybe I need to make him a better offer, because even though I don't really believe in God, I still sort of feel like he might be listening. "Okay, God? I'm going to make you a better offer, okay? I'm going to make a once-in-a-lifetime offer here, okay? This is a pretty sweet deal, so you'd better be listening. If you move this Ping-Pong ball a quarter of an inch, if you move it just a little bit, I will devote the rest of my life to you, okay?"

I'm a little nervous that he might actually do something. I stare at the Ping-Pong ball, waiting for it to move. I really hope it moves. I really hope that God exists and that he's up there in heaven and looking down on me, and that he cares about me. I don't understand why he doesn't move the Ping-Pong ball. It would be so easy for him. I mean, he parted the Red Sea, right? All I'm asking is for him to move a stinking Ping-Pong ball that weighs less than an ounce.

"Jesus, God, move the Ping-Pong ball already. Come on. Move it. It's not that big of a deal."

The Ping-Pong ball doesn't move, and I stand up and walk across the room. For a moment, I think that the Ping-Pong ball might have moved while I had my back to it. I turn and look at it. Nothing.

Shit, that was the deal of the century, if you ask me. My whole life of service for a quarter of an inch. Whatever. God can do his own thing and ignore me if he wants, but that's retarded.

I have a Bible on the bookshelf that I've never read. Somebody gave it to me as a gift after everything happened.

I pick it up and flip through part of it. I don't get it—what does everybody see in this book? It doesn't even make sense.

I open the window to my bedroom and climb out onto the roof. I like sitting up here sometimes. It's a good feeling, being up here and being isolated from everything. Nobody knows I'm here. I can't even see any other houses from here.

I look down at the pool. I wonder if I could jump from here to the pool? No, probably not. I'd probably land on the concrete and break my leg.

Why did this happen to us? Why did this happen to my brother? Why did this happen to me? It doesn't make any sense. Nothing makes any sense. How can there be a God if he would do this to me?

I still have the Bible in my hand. I stand up, holding on to the gutter to steady myself, and wing the Bible side-arm from the rooftop. It spins like a Frisbee and lands in the deep end.

That's funny. It floats. Look at that. Who would have thought that the Bible floats? Wait, wait, no it doesn't, it sinks. It definitely is sinking into the deep end of the pool.

Okay, well, I should probably get that out of there before my parents get home.

I walk over the shingles to the edge of the roof. Man, it looks a lot higher from up here. I'm not afraid of heights, but being twelve feet from the ground looking down, it looks like a long way.

Wouldn't it be ironic if God pushed me off the roof and

killed me right now? Wait, I'm not sure that would be ironic. I think *irony* is one of those words that people mess up all the time. I'll have to look up *irony* when I go back inside.

Okay, enough of this. I'm going back inside.

I go downstairs and put a Rolling Stones CD in the stereo. I turn it up. Way up. Way past the line that Mom drew in Wite-Out to mark where the stereo should never be turned past. The drums kick in on the first track and it's so loud, I can feel the bass in my backbone. God damn, that sounds good. It's almost too loud. I bet the speakers are going to blow any second. I don't care. Fuck it.

My ears are hurting, so I go into the kitchen and open the refrigerator. We don't have anything to eat. What is that about? Why can't we get any food in this house? Jesus.

All we've got is some bologna and a half gallon of two-percent milk. I fish out some American cheese singles too. I unwrap the singles and roll them up with the bologna. This is like the best snack a person can have. It's awesome. I'm nodding my head, listening to the music, eating bologna and American cheese.

Fuck it. I'm going up there.

I walk down the hall toward my brother's bedroom. They gave him his own room over the two-car garage. Behind this door and up a little set of stairs. I've never even been in here. My parents moved all his stuff in here.

I open the door and walk up the stairs. Wow. This is weird. There's a bed with a comforter on it, like he's going to come back any moment and get into bed. My mother must have done that, because it's perfectly made.

Even from up here, I can hear the opening guitar on "Gimme Shelter." I can't hear the words, but, man, that is an awesome song.

All his stuff is still in boxes, closed and taped up with his name written on them in thick black marker. I want to open up some of the boxes and see what's in there.

All of a sudden the Rolling Stones music is too frantic. I want quiet, but I also don't want to go back down there. I might not have the guts to come back. I shut the door at the bottom of the stairs with my foot. It slams shut and the music is muffled by the door. Okay. I'm ready.

I tear the packing tape off the first box I see. It rips the cardboard on top of the box, but the flaps pop open, like that's what they wanted to do the whole time.

I have a little bit of a sick feeling in my stomach. I'm not sure what I'm going to find in here. It's a box of his old football cards. He used to be crazy about collecting these things. He'd never let me touch them.

I open the next box. It's clothes. I remember this shirt; he used to wear it all the time. It still smells like him. It probably would fit me now, but I don't want to wear his clothes. I can almost see him in it.

I open the next box. This is interesting. It's the tape recorder that my parents got him for Christmas a few years ago. I wonder if the batteries still work. There's a tape in there too. Hold on, let's see what's on the tape.

*"Pass the butter."* He used to bring the tape recorder with him everywhere when he first got it. He would even bring it

to the dinner table, and that's what this is. I can hear the plates and the knives and the ice in the glasses.

"Mr. Garrison is such a loser. He's, like, totally impossible to deal with. He keeps loading us up with homework and all this reading and then on top of that he's assigning this book report, which is due next Monday."

It's him. It's my brother, Sean. He sounds exactly like himself. It's just like every other dinner-table conversation. He's just talking about himself.

"Tom said he wants me to come to his house next Friday for a sleepover."

"Who's going to be there?"

"Everybody."

"Girls?" That's my mom. She would say that.

"No, Mom, not girls. It's a sleepover."

"Well, I'm going to have to call Tom's mother and ask if there will be parental supervision."

"Oh, come on. Is that really necessary? I mean, I've known him since we were in preschool—it's not like we're going to start a riot."

"So what's the problem with calling his mother?"

"Nothing, it's just you two are so overprotective. It's not like I'm a kid anymore. I mean, I can drive now. I can go out whenever I want—you don't have to treat me like a baby."

"Sean, we're hardly treating you like a baby. I'll just call Mrs. Dickens—"

"Well, you can't call her, because she's on a trip."

"Where is she?"

*"I don't know where she is. She's on a trip. It's not like I'm her travel agent. She's coming home on Friday."*

*"She's coming home on Friday and she really wants to have a bunch of teenage boys over at her house for a sleepover?"*

*"Oh my God, Mom. You're acting like this is the biggest deal. Just let it go. God, you're so stupid."*

*"Don't call your mother stupid."*

*"I didn't. I said she was being stupid. I didn't say she was stupid. Besides, I was joking."*

*"Well, don't say she's being stupid. She's just looking out for you."*

*"I don't need anyone to look out for me. I'm practically an adult—"*

I stop the tape. I feel like I'm going to throw up and like I'm going to cry at the same time. Just from hearing his voice. Just from hearing the way he talked. He sounded so real on that tape. He sounded just like himself.

I can't stand it. I really might throw up. I go downstairs to the bathroom and kneel in front of the toilet. I think I'm going to throw up. Wait. No. My head is getting lighter. I can only see white. There are sparkles in my eyes.

I'm staring at the ceiling. Where am I? Am I in a hospital? Am I in bed? Where am I?

Oh, I'm in the bathroom. I think I passed out. I felt like I was going to throw up, but then I must have passed out in the bathroom.

My head is throbbing and there are these white sparkles

in my eyes still. I think I might have hit my head on something.

I put one hand on the sink and the other on the top of the toilet. I pull myself up to standing. There's a big red spot on the side of my head. Jesus, I think I hit it pretty hard. Wasn't there music playing before? Now there's no music. I wonder if I'm deaf.

I want to lie down somewhere, but I don't want to go back into my brother's room. I hold on to the door and then the kitchen table and then the wall, and then I get to the stairs leading up to my room. There are too many stairs. I don't think I'm going to be able to walk up all of these stairs. I get down on my hands and knees and crawl.

It's a long way to crawl, but I get all the way into my bedroom and climb up into my bed.

God damn it, I want to cry. I wish I could cry, but I can't. I can't cry. No matter how hard I try. No matter how many sad things I think about, I can't cry. Jesus, what's wrong with me?

Fuck. Why can't I cry? What's wrong with me? There are ten million things in my head right now, and I can't get my mind around any of them. Jesus, the more I think about things, the more I can't even start to think about any of them.

I feel like I'm choking on my own brain.

Mom and Dad are home. I hear them moving around downstairs. Shit, I think I fell asleep again. Well, at least my head is feeling better. That's something.

I get up and go downstairs. I must have slept a long time, because now it's dinner. Dad's outside working the grill. It looks like pork chops.

It's my job to set the table. I pick up four plates out of the cupboard. I don't know why I do that. I put one back.

I make sure to only get three knives, forks, and spoons out of the silverware drawer. I get some place mats off the top of the refrigerator. The blue ones. I like those.

On a warm day like this we eat out on the screened-in porch, which is good, because one side of the table is pushed against the screen. So there's only room for three people.

I fold some paper napkins diagonally and put them under the forks, on the left side. Dad brings in the pork chops off the grill and puts them down in the center of the table. He seems like he's got something on his mind, because normally he would have said something to me.

Mom brings out a basket of crescent rolls and a jar of applesauce—economy size. Wow, that is a lot of applesauce. I wonder how many apples they had to kill to fill that jar—probably about a million. People for the Ethical Treatment of Apples is going to form a protest outside our house.

Why did she buy so much applesauce? Seriously, there are only three of us now. What was she thinking? God, that's exactly the kind of shit that pisses me off.

I sit down at my place and they sit at theirs. No one says anything about anything. I just look down at my pork chop and try to cut it into little pieces. The meat is tougher than it should be. I think my dad cooked it for too long.

Mom says, "Who wants applesauce?"

I look up at her. What the hell is she talking about? Why would I want to eat that applesauce? I don't want to encourage her crazy purchasing of giant quantities of food for three people.

I don't say anything. I don't want any, but if I say that, then I'll have to tell her why, and I don't want to do that. That would be bad. So I don't say anything at all. My dad takes some applesauce, and then they both look at me like they're expecting me to take some too.

She says, "Wanna try some applesauce, bud?"

See, that's what I hate about her. I hate it when she talks like a baby for no reason. That's so fucking annoying. Wanna? Who says that?

I still don't answer. She asks again, louder this time, as if I didn't hear her. "Want some applesauce, Brian?"

Now I'm just not going to answer out of principle. Does she think I can't hear her? If I wanted applesauce, I'd take it. I'm not fucking paralyzed. Jesus.

"Applesauce?"

Come on. She can't seriously still be asking me about applesauce. What is that?

"It's chunky."

I look up at her, directly in her eyes, and I try to show, just with my eyes, how little I care about what she's saying.

She's so crazy. Why is she obsessed with applesauce all of a sudden?

At first I was kind of joking. I just wanted to see how long I could hold out with the no-answering thing, but now, because she's gotten so obsessed with applesauce, I've realized that I'm never going to talk to her ever again. Never—not in my lifetime.

Dad has been sitting quietly, cutting up his nasty dried-out pork chop one piece at a time and dipping it into his chunky applesauce. He's doing it so slowly and carefully. If you didn't know him you probably wouldn't be able to see that he's angry.

But I can tell that he's just burning up inside. I can tell by how slowly he's eating. How he's taking his time chewing the pork chops on one side of his mouth and then moving the clumpy meat to the other side. He's not gnashing into it, like he would if things were normal.

I stare down at my plate and cut the meat with my knife in my right hand and feed myself with my fork in my left hand, just like the Europeans do it. I wish I was European. I would probably get better food for dinner.

You know what would make this meat taste a little better? Applesauce. It would moisten it up a little. Because the way Dad cooked this pork chop, it's just so dry. Of course, now that I've gotten into this thing where I don't like applesauce, I can't be all like, Wow, applesauce would go great with this meal, Mom, you were right. Fuck that. I'm not saying that.

I cut one more dry little piece and chew it up. I have to take a big drink of milk to swallow it. Shit, that's some dry shit.

Mom is watching me eat. Don't ask. Don't ask, Mom. I'm warning you. Don't ask.

"Want some applesauce, bud? It's chunky."

Jesus. I look up and sign "Shut up" right at her.

Dad picks up a crescent roll and wings it at me from across the table. It's not a very good throw, because it bounces on the table in front of me and splatters me with pork chop.

I stand up and scream at him, "What the hell was that? What the hell was that?"

He screams back, "Don't you dare give my wife the finger!"

"I didn't!" It must have looked like it, but I didn't.

I'm not sitting at this table anymore. I leave the porch and go upstairs to my room. I slam the door so hard I think I hear the foundation crack.

I go into the bathroom and look at myself. God damn, I don't think I've ever seen myself so angry. God damn.

I think I see a tear in my eye. I focus on it in the mirror and try to get it to roll down my face. I want to cry. I want to see myself cry, but there's something inside me that's blocking all the tears from coming out. It's like all the moisture in the world has been sucked out of me.

Fuck it. It's not worth it.

I go back to my bed and put my face down in my pillows. I scream as loud as I can into the pillows, but it hardly makes any noise at all. I wait a second and let all the anger roll into a tight ball inside me, and then I push it up and out of my lungs and into the pillow.

I just heard someone in the hallway. What are they

doing out there? Are they listening to me? What are they doing?

I think I hear a light rapping on the door, like a knock, but so light and timid, it's hard to even know if that's what it was. I can tell by the footsteps that it's my mother out there. Her footsteps are soft and tentative. If my dad was out there, he would sound like a giant.

Something is being slipped under the door. It's a note. Who slips a note under the door?

I get up and pick up the note. It's my mother's handwriting.

> We don't understand what happened at dinner.
> We would like to talk to you about it.
> Love,
> Mom and Dad
> P.S. Why was there a Bible in the pool?

# TWENTY-ONE

I have to break up with Monica. We're not right for each other. So I've decided that I need to break up with her, but I feel terrible that I have to tell her. The thing is that I've never broken up with anyone before, so I don't really know what I'm doing.

We're sitting in the living room, where the stereo is. I put on a CD that she really likes, and she's singing along with the lyrics. I was going to tell her that we weren't right for each other right away, but I can't make myself say it. Besides, she's singing, so I don't want to interrupt her.

She really doesn't have a very good singing voice, but she thinks she does. I grab the remote control and pause the CD right in the middle of her singing.

149

She freezes, like we're playing some sort of musical-chairs-type game, and I press play again. She starts singing with the music again, just where it left off.

I pause it again, because I really want to tell her that I want to break up with her, but she thinks it's a game now, so she stops herself mid-lyric and freezes like a statue.

I want her to be normal. I want her to act like herself so I can just break up with her and get it over with, so I fast-forward toward the end of the song.

The music flickers through the speakers, and Monica sings with it as best she can. I guess she really likes this song and wants to sing along with it; either that or she knows I'm trying to break up with her and is trying to distract me.

I pause the song again and she freezes again. This is getting ridiculous.

I say, "What are you doing?"

"Singing."

"Yeah, but why?"

"It's fun. Why? Do you want to say something?"

I don't know what to say. So I'm just quiet for a long time, and she reaches over to take the remote control from me.

I can't let this go on. I say, "Did you ever think that . . . maybe you and I are . . . I mean, did you ever wonder if . . . I mean, since we're so . . ."

I can't finish my sentences, because I can't make myself say the words that are going to hurt her. I don't want her to think I'm a bad person. I don't want her to know that I haven't been in love with her for a long time.

Maybe she knows what I am going to say, or maybe she doesn't, but anyway, she's singing to herself even though the CD is paused.

I can't take it anymore, her singing, so I just blurt out, "I think we should break up."

She pretends like she didn't hear me, and she keeps singing, and so I have to say it again.

The second time I say it, she stops singing and looks at me like I've broken her heart. Then she starts crying.

I feel so bad that I made her cry. I hate watching her face turn red and blotchy, so I hold her head against my shoulder and hug her and try to make her feel better.

She stops crying, which makes me feel better, and says, "If I spend less time with my friends, can we stay together?"

I guess I used to complain that she spent too much time with Molly and not enough with me, but I don't care about that anymore, so I say, "No."

She says, "If I don't talk about politics, can we stay together?"

I don't know how she knew that I hated it when she talked about politics, but I think about it and I decide that it wouldn't have made a difference, so I say, "No."

She says, "If I shave my legs, can we stay together?"

That was silly. "No."

She says, "I just hope we can still be friends."

"Me too," I say, even though I'm not sure if I really mean it.

She says, "Do you still want to be friends?"

Honestly, I really don't. I don't like being around her. I don't like talking to her. I don't really like anything about her. I just want her to leave.

I know I shouldn't say no to that question. But I also don't feel like lying. I don't say no. I say, "Maybe."

# TWENTY-TWO

The whole cast of the play is on our silent retreat. We get to spend this whole weekend in a fancy hotel pretending we're deaf.

Our first goal is to see if we can communicate with other people, not just the people we're acting with. Kathy gave us all pens and pads so if we have to we can write something down for the people we're trying to communicate with. So Dan, Amy, Cheryl, and I all walk over to the mall across the street from the hotel.

Dan and I are walking together, trying to talk in sign language. I've gotten pretty good at signing what I mean, but it's a lot harder to tell what other people are signing.

I sign, "What music?" to Dan. I'm trying to ask what the song is on the radio here in the mall.

He signs back, "What?"

"Music. What?"

"Song? Sing?"

"No. Music."

"What?"

"This song. Man sound Police." I'm trying to say that the singer in this band sounds like Sting when he was in the Police.

Dan shakes his head. I guess we're not going to be having a very long conversation today.

He heads off toward the food court and I walk over to a sporting-goods store and find a woman standing out front.

I sign, "Hello."

She doesn't do anything. She's just looking at me, trying to figure out why I'm using sign language.

I sign, "Where music?" Meaning, where is the music store?

She says, "What?"

I sign, "Me deaf. No talk. Where music?"

"What?"

I sign, "Music up? Music down? Music left? Right?"

She says, "I don't know what you're saying. Here, write it down."

She seems mad at me for some reason.

I write down *music store* on my paper and show it to her. She looks at it and then looks at me pretty skeptically and says, "I don't know."

I point to the paper again and try signing again, but she pushes the paper away and says really loudly, "I don't know!"

I walk away. I didn't expect her to get so mad at me. That was a weird experience. Maybe I should have asked where to find a candy store or something.

Dan, Amy, Cheryl, and I are sitting in the hot tub in the hotel. This is such a nice hotel. I can't believe we get to stay here. I'm so tired, though. I'm so sick of trying to do sign language. It's so hard to get other people to try to understand you, and to try to understand other people. It's like there's all these layers between everyone. Like we're all in the middle of a blizzard and we're bundled up in our coats and scarves and hats, and no one can hear or say anything.

Except we're not in a blizzard, we're in a hot tub.

I'm so tired, I didn't even realize how weird it is to be in the hot tub with these three people. Shit, now I'm starting to get uncomfortable.

Amy is signing something. God, she's so good at signing. She's so fast, I can't even begin to understand what she's signing. Dan is nodding his fist, the sign for "yes," and so is Cheryl. Okay, what's going on? I should be paying better attention.

Amy signs something directly to me. I recognize the sign for "true," but not the second sign she does. She finger-spells it for me. "D-A-R-E."

Oh shit. She wants to play Truth or Dare here in the hot tub? Wow, that's kind of gutsy, because there are still some other people around.

Amy signs, "I first. Dan. Truth? Dare?"

Dan signs, "Truth."

"What you best kiss?"

Dan signs, "You. Me. First."

Amy puts her hand over her heart, like she's touched by that. Cheryl and I look away.

Dan's turn. He chooses Cheryl. "Cheryl. Truth? Dare?"

"Truth."

"What you big afraid?"

"Me big afraid . . ." She puts her head almost all the way underwater, so just her eyes are above water, and makes a face like she's drowning. We all nod like we understand.

Cheryl signs to me. "Truth? Dare?"

Shit. I don't want to tell them anything. "Dare."

"Dare? Okay. You run around pool."

"Okay." I start to get up out of the hot tub, but Dan stops me.

He signs, "No. You N-U-D-E run around pool."

Oh, I must have missed that sign. I look around. There's still a woman cleaning up, folding towels and straightening the deck chairs. I can't do this, I'll get arrested.

I sit back in the hot tub. I sign, "Okay. Truth."

Cheryl signs, "Who you sex first?"

Shit. I don't want to, but I have to tell the truth.

I sign, "I no sex first."

Dan signs, "You no sex? Never?"

"No. Never."

They all look away for a second, like they're embarrassed

for me. It's my turn. I guess I get to ask Amy something. She smiles at me and signs, "Truth," before I even ask her.

I sign, "When you sex first?"

"Who or when?"

"Who? When? Where? What? Why?"

Everyone laughs silently at that.

Amy signs, "I sex first time Dan. We sex first time at you house."

"Me house?"

"Yes. You, me drink. Dan, me sex." Oh my God, she and Dan had sex for the first time in my bathroom that night we got drunk? That is fucking disturbing.

Amy signs to Cheryl, "How many people you sex?"

"Me sex four people."

Cheryl signs to Dan, "How many people you sex?"

Dan looks right in her eyes like he wants to strangle her and then signs, "Me sex one. Amy." I can't believe he lied. I mean, I understand why he did, but I didn't think you were allowed to lie in Truth or Dare.

This is getting really uncomfortable. I can feel everyone getting tense. Dan turns to me and signs, "What you worst time?"

I think he's asking me what the worst moment of my life was, but I pretend not to understand. Why would he do that? Is he turning on me just because Cheryl made him uncomfortable?

I sign, "What?"

"What worst time you? You have worst time?"

I shake my head like I don't know what he's talking about. I'm not going to sit here and be interrogated by Dan in sign language.

I sign, "Me tired. Me sleep. No more play." And I get out of the hot tub, grab a towel, and go back to the room.

# TWENTY-THREE

Opening night. I'm not nervous. I know who my character is. I know my lines. I know how he talks. I can do this.

I'm in the second scene, right after Dan and Amy have their fight onstage. Then I come out and do my speech-therapy scene with Dan. The whole play is supposed to take place in Dan's character's head, so the rest of us just kind of go in and out of the darkness, but he has to be onstage for the whole time.

I'm standing in the wings and the curtains are already open. Our whole set is black and you can't really see any-thing when there are no lights on, but I can see the audience because of the exit lights.

There are so many people out there. I can see their faces. I wonder where my parents are.

All we're waiting on now is for Dan to come out onstage, and then Amy will come out and do her sign language, and then Dan will do his monologue, and then it's my scene, but for some reason Dan isn't here.

Someone comes up to me, taps me on the shoulder, and whispers, "Where's Dan?"

"I don't know."

"Have you seen him?"

"No."

"Help me find him."

I start looking around. I saw him earlier getting his makeup on, but I haven't seen him since then.

The audience is rustling around out there. I can hear them mumbling and coughing. They're waiting for something to happen.

The crew is hustling around backstage looking for Dan. Becky, the stage manager, motions for Amy to go onstage alone. She can't go onstage without Dan—the whole play takes place in his brain.

She turns and looks at me as if to say, Whatever happens, don't leave me out there.

I peek out at the audience again. People are talking to each other. Something has got to happen.

I wonder if I should go out onstage and start improvising something. Maybe that would be a good idea. What would I do? Pretend that I'm Dan? I don't know his lines. Maybe I could think of something to say.

Is that what I should do?

Amy walks out onstage by herself and stands center stage and the lights come up on her. She starts her sign language monologue. Where is Dan? This can't happen. Where is he?

There's Dan. He's coming out of the dressing room. What was he doing, taking a nap? Cheryl walks out of the dressing room.

Dan's face is flushed, but he walks out onstage right after Amy and delivers his line. *"She went away from me. Or did I drive her away?"*

# TWENTY-FOUR

Amy found out. I don't know how she found out, but she did. It happened after our final performance. We were all taking our makeup off and getting out of our costumes. I love that about the theater, that the boys and girls change in the same dressing room. God, I've seen so many bras and panties in the past three days. It's awesome.

Anyway, all I know is that Amy wasn't in the dressing room while I was changing. She was somewhere talking to someone. She came stomping backstage, crying like a little kid who can't get enough air.

Dan went running after her. He must have known what had happened. He must have sensed that she'd found out.

They went out the back door and stood in the parking

lot, fighting. I watched through the window. She wasn't crying anymore. He was crying. He was bent over, hugging her, with his arms around her waist and his head near her stomach. She was standing with her arms at her sides.

She must have been in shock. She must have been totally in shock, because there wasn't any expression on her face. He kept holding on to her, his arms wrapped around her waist and his head buried in her stomach. He must have been saying something that made her feel sorry for him. He must have said something, because she took one hand and patted his head, like a person petting a dog who doesn't like dogs very much.

I couldn't watch anymore. I felt sorry for her, because she looked so sad and so cold at the same time. I'd never seen her face look like that before.

I felt sorry for him too, because he looked so pathetic and weak, and I'd never seen him look weak before.

Dan asks me to walk him out to his car. I don't know why. The last time we really talked was that night in the hot tub. We've pretty much stopped being friends, he and I. Which is fine with me. I've had enough.

We walk out to his car, shoulder to shoulder. He's not saying anything, and neither am I. There's just nothing that I want to say to him.

We stop next to his car and he turns toward me. He's a few inches taller than I am. His skin is pale and he should really shave off that gross red goatee.

He says, "If you hit on Amy, I'll kill you."

He gets into his car and drives off.

I can't believe he said that. I can't believe he asked me to walk him out to his car just so he could say that to me. What an asshole. What a fucking asshole.

# TWENTY-FIVE

Is it in? I think it's in.

It's in. It's definitely in, and I'm moving it around, just like I practiced. Okay, I'm moving it back and forth I think that's the right way to do it.

She's not doing anything. I think she's holding her breath.

Is this right? Am I doing it right?

I open my eyes and look across the room. The red digital clock. The dresser. The *Reservoir Dogs* poster.

I'm going to remember this moment for the rest of my life. I'm going to always remember everything about this moment.

Shit.

Amy and I are lying in the dark, talking. She says, "Do you regret it?"

"No. Do you?"

"No. I think I just realized something about myself, though."

"What?"

"Nothing. I'll tell you later. It's just random."

"What is it?"

"Nothing."

"What?"

"Nothing. I'll tell you later."

"Okay."

Neither one of us says anything for a long time. It's dark. There's darkness everywhere.

She rolls on one side, facing me. She runs her finger down the side of my face, all the way from my eye down to my lip. She says, "How come your brother is never around?"

"My brother?"

"Yeah, where is he? You mentioned him once, but you never talk about him."

"I don't?" I know that I don't.

"No."

"Do you want to know?"

"Only if you want to tell me."

"I'll tell you, but you have to promise not to tell anyone else, okay?"

"Okay. I promise."

"Not even Dan."

"Especially not Dan."

"Okay, I'm going to tell you."

"You don't have to."

"I want to."

"You sure?"

"Yeah . . . I just have to get up my nerve."

"You don't—"

"Hold on. Just give me a minute." I'm thinking through all the words and the way to say them. I'm plotting them out like I'm about to climb Everest.

The words don't connect when I think them in my head—they're just words. I have to say them out loud in order for them to make any sense. I have to say them out loud.

*All right, start in the . . .* Finish the sentence! *Start in the beginning.*

"My brother got a car—and it was a pretty cool car, but it was kind of old—I mean, it didn't have air bags or anything."

I stop and take a breath. That was hard, but that wasn't even the hardest part.

I kind of expect her to ask a question, but she's just looking at me and being sympathetic. And then I just start talking.

"So . . . he's only a year and a half older than me, so I was kind of pissed when he got a car. But he was pretty cool about it. He would drive me home from school sometimes. We used to go the long way home sometimes, and sometimes we'd go out and drive on these country roads where almost nobody lived.

"It was cool, because he could really get the car going on those roads—you know, because they were so straight and smooth. And they had these little hills, sometimes, where you'd feel like you were on a roller coaster if you were going really fast. Anyway . . ."

I stop and take a deep breath. My mouth is so dry. I wish I had a glass of water.

Amy touches my arm. That helps. That makes this easier. I take another deep breath and say, "A couple of months after my brother got this car, he went out to this party—with his friends. And I guess he maybe had a couple of beers or something and . . .

"He was supposed to be home by midnight . . . and my mom was waiting up for him . . . but he never came home. . . ."

I'm crying. There are tears coming out of my face. Where did those come from?

"They found him on that old country road that we used to drive on. They said he was going at least seventy when the car went off the road. And he didn't have his headlights on, so no one saw the car in the ditch for a long time. . . ."

I'm crying so hard now that I can't get my words out.

"And he . . . wasn't . . . wearing . . . his . . . seat belt. . . ."

I can't say any more words. I'm just crying now. I put my face in Amy's hair and hold on to her with my arms. She holds on to me and I hold on to her.

This is what I've been waiting for. This is what I wanted. I just wanted to say it out loud.

I finally stopped crying. Where was all that? Was it inside me?

Amy and I haven't said anything for about a half an hour. I'm so happy it was her. I'm so happy I told her before I told anyone else. She's so perfect and so kind. She's just exactly the right girl for me. I'm so lucky that things turned out like this.

"Brian?"

"Yeah?"

"Are you awake?"

"Yeah."

"You remember that thing I was going to tell you later?"

"Yeah. That thing from before."

"Mm-hmm. I think I should tell you now."

"Okay. Tell me anything."

"You might not like it, though."

"You can tell me anything."

"You sure?"

"Yeah."

"Promise you're not going to be mad."

"Okay."

"Promise."

"I promise."

"Okay." She doesn't say anything.

"What is it?"

"Nothing."

"Seriously, what is it?" I'm starting to get nervous.

"It's just . . ."

"What?"

"It's just that I . . ."

"What?" I'm getting frustrated.

"It's just that I realized . . ."

"Come on. You can tell me anything."

"It's just that I realized that I'm still in love with Dan."

I don't say anything. That was the last thing I thought she would say. She puts her clothes on and leaves.

# TWENTY-SIX

**I**'m all alone. I don't have anyone and I don't care about anyone and no one cares about me. My parents don't love me and my brother doesn't love me and none of my friends love me and I'm all alone.

Why does it have to be like this? I wish I could just jump off the roof or drive my car into a tree, but I can't.

I can't because I'm too fucking afraid.

God damn it. Why am I stuck in this skin? Why am I stuck here? Why couldn't I have gone to that party with him and driven him home?

I don't understand why my life turned out like this. I can't get my fucking head around it.

I just want to sleep.

I wake up and I feel a hand between my shoulder blades. It takes me a few seconds to figure out where I am. I'm in my room, and I'm lying on my bed, but I'm dressed and it's light out. Is it morning? Evening? What happened?

Whose hand is on my back? It feels like my brother's hand, but it can't be. I want it to be. I want it to be so badly, but it's not. I know it's not, but I want it to be.

I want him to be here and I want to tell him that I'm sorry for everything. I want him to say that he misses me as much as I miss him.

God, I miss him so much.

I turn over and look at my dad's face. He looks like my brother when you look just at his eyes. They both have blue eyes, but my dad has a beard.

I'm still not really sure if it's morning or night. I can't tell. I think it's night now, because I smell dinner cooking.

My dad is just looking at me and not saying anything. His hand is on my shoulder and he's not moving it. He's actually holding on to my shoulder pretty tightly. He's holding on to me like he doesn't want me to slip away.

I see his eyes looking at my face, but it doesn't feel like he's seeing me. It feels like he's looking for something. Maybe when he looks at me he sees my brother, just like I do when I look at him.

He looks at my face and I look at his, and he holds on to my shoulder and he's not letting go, and I don't want him to either.

172

I go downstairs with my dad for dinner. We sit down next to each other at the dining-room table. We don't sit in the seats that we normally sit in. He doesn't sit in the big chair at one end of the table, and I don't sit in the smaller chair at the other end. Instead, we both move our places and sit on one side of the table in chairs right next to each other.

We're actually sitting on the side of the table that Mom usually sits on, so she sits across from us, where my brother used to sit. It still feels weird that there are only three of us now, but at least we're not leaving the big empty hole anymore.

No one has to say anything. It doesn't matter if anyone says anything. We're all thinking and feeling the same things.

# TWENTY-SEVEN

I'm sitting in front of the theater by myself. Sitting on the metal rail with my feet on the railing below and my fist under my chin. I bet I totally look like that statue of the guy who is thinking, except he probably wasn't thinking about how he'd just had sex with his ex-friend's girlfriend. Although, who knows, maybe he was.

This is so weird. Everyone has been treating me so weird. It's like everyone knows what happened with Amy, but I don't know how they would, because I didn't tell anyone.

Maybe no one knows. Maybe everyone is just treating me normally, and I'm the one who's acting weird.

It's eating me up inside. That whole thing with Amy. I

don't know—I guess I wanted it to be more special, or I wanted it to be different. I wanted everything to open up and change colors and smells so I would walk out into the world and everything would be different.

Now everyone is treating me differently, but it's not like I pictured. Everyone is just ignoring me for some reason. I can't believe that Amy would tell everyone—because I know that she didn't want anyone to know.

I hear people, but I'm not going to look at them. I'm not going to look at anyone. I guess I just want to be by myself. I don't need anyone or anything.

What the fuck was that? Somebody just came up behind me and smeared something on me. Dan? What the hell?

I look at my back and there's something sticky all over my favorite jacket. What the fuck?

"What the fuck?"

"Fuck you, you dick."

"What?"

"Fuck you." Dan runs right at me and tackles me. I fall back and onto the ground. I'm on my back. Fuck. I've got to get off my back. My brother and I used to wrestle all the time. We used to wrestle, ever since we were really little.

I slip my legs out from underneath him and use my leverage to flip him off me and onto his back. I sit up on his chest and hold my fist up like I'm going to punch him. He pulls his hands up to cover his face.

I can't hit him. I can't fucking hit him.

Someone really strong with huge arms pulls me off him

like I weigh as much as a Frisbee. It's Clarence—the security guard. He holds me by my neck and marches me and Dan down to the office.

Fuck, this is exactly what I don't need.

Dan and I are sitting in Mr. Scott's office. He's staring at us, trying to figure out what happened between us. Honestly, I can't even remember. I used to like Dan. I used to like him, but now I can't even look at him.

Mr. Scott says, "So, you guys want to talk about what happened?"

I'm not going to say anything, and I don't think Dan is going to say anything either. This isn't something that we need to talk about in front of Mr. Scott.

"All right. If you guys aren't going to say anything, I'm going to give you an option. Either you can both take a suspension . . . or . . ."

Dan and I both look up at Mr. Scott. The last thing I want is to get in trouble at school and have to explain it to my parents. Especially for something like this.

We're waiting for Mr. Scott to finish his sentence. "Or . . . we can find another way to settle this conflict."

Dan speaks up. "Like what?"

"Like a game of checkers."

What? Is he serious? Is he giving us a choice between being suspended from school or playing a game of checkers? That is a really easy decision.

I say, "I think checkers could work."

"Dan?"

"Yeah, checkers."

"Right. Okay. Good choice. You two sit here and face each other and play a few games of checkers."

I take red and Dan takes black.

He says, "Who goes first?"

"Smoke comes before fire."

# TWENTY-EIGHT

I can't believe I'm still in Chorus. I can't believe I signed up for this shit. I'm wearing a fucking sequined vest and I'm standing in the middle of an old-folks' home singing the love theme from *Phantom of the Opera* at eight o'clock on a Friday night.

If there is a God, I don't know why he didn't get me out of this.

I'm moving my lips, but there's no sound coming out. I can't bear to really sing, because this song is so stupid. Tremulous and tender.

What a fucking joke. The old people don't even care. They're just trying to figure out how to chew the chicken that's in front of them. They don't care about a singing group from a local high school butchering an Andrew Lloyd Webber score.

I have never felt more meaningless and stupid than I do right now.

If it weren't for Katya, this chorus would totally suck. She's carrying all of us on her back, singing her heart out.

After the performance, she comes up to me and says, "You were great."

"What?" I say. "I didn't even do anything."

"I know, I mean you were great in that play a couple of weeks ago."

"Oh. Thanks."

"Yeah, it was amazing. I mean, I didn't know you knew sign language."

"Yeah, well, it's not as hard as singing."

She says, "Listen, um, some friends and I are going down to the beach to hang out. Do you have any interest in doing that?"

"Yeah. I'd like that."

"Okay, um, could you give me a ride, maybe?"

"Sure."

Wow, did Katya just ask me to go out?

I open the car door for her and then head over to the other side. She unlocks my door for me, just like the guy in A Bronx Tale says she should. All right. She's a good woman.

I say, "You hungry?"

179

"Absolutely. I love to eat."

I laugh. You hardly ever hear a girl say she loves to eat. God, she's attractive.

"What do you want?" I'm thinking McDonald's or Taco Bell.

She says, "You know, there's this little Italian place on the way to the beach that I've always wanted to try. You know the one with the Japanese lanterns out front?"

She wants to go out to eat? This really is a date. I say, "Great. Let's do it."

She shows me how to get there, and we park out front. She lets me open her door for her. She's not like Monica— she doesn't have a problem with me being nice to her.

We're the only couple in this restaurant, because it's kind of late, and the waitress is this old Italian woman who obviously thinks we're really cute.

The table is a little too big and we're sitting in these giant leather chairs with armrests and metal rivets holding the leather on. I sink into the chair and I have to keep sitting up to be able to reach my drink.

I look up and Katya is smiling at me, like she's just about to start laughing, and I can't help it, I start smiling too. She giggles a little and then I start laughing. It actually is kind of funny that we're sitting here in this Italian restaurant all by ourselves. I bet they have a bowl full of mints with a little metal spoon on the way out of the restaurant. What are we doing here?

I say, "This is a little bizarre, isn't it?"

"Yeah, it is, but I love it."

The waitress comes back and we order. Katya gets the eggplant Parmesan and I order the fettuccini Alfredo.

Someone dims the lights and Katya and I lean in closer to each other. Now we're getting romantic. This is better.

I say, "What's your favorite band?"

"Favorite band or favorite singer?"

"Uh, whichever."

"Elvis, by far."

"Are you serious? I love Elvis. Elvis Presley, right?"

"Of course."

"Wow, you are so cool. What's your favorite song?"

"God, there are so many. 'Are You Lonesome Tonight?' "

"Oh my God. That is an amazing song."

We both start singing the chorus in fairly respectable Elvis impressions. I laugh. She's a fun date. How many girls will sing "Are You Lonesome Tonight?" with you at an Italian restaurant?

She says, "What about you?"

"Well, all respect to Elvis, but the Beatles are the best band in the world."

"What? I hate the Beatles."

"You hate the Beatles?"

"They're terrible. They can't sing."

"What?" I shake my head. She must be joking. Nobody hates the Beatles.

"They are so overrated. And I can't stand that whole British nasal voice they all sing in."

"Oh my God. You hate the Beatles."

"Yeah, what's that song about 'Love Me Do'? That is a stupid song. All their songs suck."

"Whoa, you can't say that. You cannot say that all Beatles songs suck. What about 'A Day in the Life'? What about 'Don't Let Me Down'? What about 'She Came in Through the Bathroom Window'?"

"I don't know those. All I know is Please Please Please Please Me, She Loves Me, She Loves You, I Love Her, You Love Me. They suck."

"Check, please."

She looks at me for a second to see if I'm serious, but I'm not serious. I couldn't walk out on her, even though she's totally wrong about the Beatles. I guess that's the first thing I'm going to have to teach her.

She can teach me about singing and I can teach her about the Beatles—that's not a totally terrible thing to base a relationship on, is it?

We get back in the car and drive together without talking, but it doesn't feel like we really need to talk. I feel comfortable with her.

I don't think I've ever felt this way with a girl before.

We park at Seventy-Ninth Street and walk out to the beach on the old boardwalk. We climb up the dune, and the ocean is getting louder as we get closer. There's a little breeze that blows some sand into my face, but I don't mind. It's a warm night.

We meet up with her friends. They're sitting in a circle

with a guitar and a little bonfire. We sit down for a while, and she sings along with the songs they're playing.

The way she just closes her eyes and lets all her feelings roll right out of her—my God, that's something to see. She's so raw. So real.

After a while, she whispers in my ear, "Do you want to get our feet wet?" And we stand up and walk away from the crowd.

The night and the moon and the music and the sound of the waves on the beach. I want everything in my life to be like this forever.

We sit down near the water and take off our shoes and bury our toes in the sand. I say, "I've never been to this part of the beach before."

She says, "The beach is so much better above Sixtieth Street."

It's a little bit hard to hear, because the waves are breaking on the beach in front of us.

I lie back and look up at the stars and she lies down next to me. We're not touching, but it feels like we are. She turns toward me and says, "Let's turn our heads so we can look up at the stars and talk at the same time."

"Okay." We turn our bodies so that our heads are right next to each other but our feet are pointing in opposite directions. Her ear is right next to my ear and all I can see are stars. Is my brother up there? Is he in heaven, or is there nothing? Is everything just gone when you go? Or is it all white linen and harps?

She says, "What are you thinking about?"

I breathe out. I'm not sure I want to tell her yet. "Oh . . . that's a long story."

"I'm not going anywhere."

"Okay, I'll tell you, but don't get up and leave, okay?"

"I won't."

"Because the last person I told, she just got up and left afterward."

"I won't do that. You can trust me with the breakables."

I start from the beginning and tell her everything. I tell her about how we used to be this normal family, and how it felt like everything was always going to be the same. I tell her about how Sean and I used to drive together on the country road, and how he went to that party and how he never came home.

I tell her every detail about how I got so angry then that I've never even been to see my brother's grave. I tell her everything and it comes out like a river this time, not like a flood.

After I'm finished, she reaches up over her head and puts her hand on the side of my face and leaves it there for a long time. I feel so close to her. I want to know everything about her. I want to lock myself in a room with her and sit and stare into her eyes and hear everything that she's ever thought. I want to listen to her sing. I want to hold her in my arms. I know it won't change what's happened, but I just want to hold her.

There's so much that we have to do. There's so much we

have to talk about. I know I've only spent a few hours with her, but I know it's the beginning of something.

I stand up. She stands up too. And we're standing in the moonlight on a beach at the edge of an ocean, and I know what we have to do right now.

I don't say anything, but I take off my shirt and she takes off her shirt. I take off my pants and she takes off her pants. I take off my underwear and she takes off hers. And we run as fast as we can into the ocean.

A wave hits me at the knees and I dive straight in. I swim out past where the waves are breaking and I wait for her. She swims out to me, and we float together in the water.

Every time we move, the water around us glows this kind of green color—like lightning bugs in the water. The glowing things are surrounding us, lighting up our bodies in the ocean. Floating.

We're not touching, but it feels like we are, together in the ocean.

We're sitting in my car outside Katya's house. I turn off the engine and we sit in the dark in a spot on the street between the streetlights.

I reach over and hold her hand. She's so cold. She's so cold from being in the ocean. I put my arm around her and she leans into me. I smell her hair and it smells so good that I'm out of breath.

I say, "Do you want to go inside?" Because it's probably much warmer inside.

She says, "No. I want to stay with you."

I want to kiss her so badly, but I also don't want to. I just want to hold her and warm her up. I want to take care of her and have her take care of me.

She's still freezing, though, even though it's not that cold out. Her lips are turning blue and her fingers are like icicles. I look around the car for a blanket or a sweatshirt or something, but I don't have any of those things.

I take off my shirt and give it to her. She smiles and puts it on over hers and snuggles into my chest. I can feel her breasts pressing against me, and I want so badly to make out with her, but I don't. I just hold her and feel her body warm up against mine.

She makes a sound like a purr of a kitten and her breathing slows down. I think she's falling asleep. I close my eyes and feel her body and my body together.

I think I might fall asleep too. I'm not really comfortable, because of the way I'm leaning against the seat belt, but I'm totally relaxed, so it's not even bothering me.

Her breathing has changed. I think she's asleep. I love this. I love that she feels safe enough to sleep in my arms.

I wake up and the windows of the car are all fogged up from our breathing, and Katya is still sound asleep in my arms. I don't know how long we've been sleeping like this together.

I move a little and she wakes up. She says, "Oh my gosh. I think I fell asleep."

I laugh. "Yeah, I think you did."

"I'm sorry. I was just so cozy."

"That's okay. I liked it."

"You did? You didn't mind?"

"No, I thought it was cute."

She looks up at me. Her face is only about an inch or two from mine and her eyes are wide open. Mine are wide open too, and I lean down and kiss her lightly on the lips.

She kisses me back, and neither one of us closes our eyes.

My head is foggy from sleeping in the car, but her lips wake me up and I want to kiss her like this forever.

She pulls back for a moment and says, "What time is it?"

"It's either really late or really early."

"Oh, my dad is going to be pissed."

"You should go?"

"You want me to go?"

"No, I want you to stay."

"How long?"

"Forever."

"How about five minutes?"

"I'll take it."

We kiss again—deeper and longer and slower than I've ever kissed anyone. It's a kiss that feels like it could go on for days. It's the only time I've ever kissed anyone that I wasn't thinking about getting on with the sex stuff.

Her arms are wrapped around my back and my hand is under her shirt, but I'm not thinking about unhooking her bra, I'm just thinking about how good her skin feels.

She presses herself against me and I press against her, and it feels like we're trying to become one person.

She pulls away and I feel like something just got amputated. "I have to go."

"Oh."

"Don't forget about me."

"Not a chance."

# TWENTY-NINE

**I**'m driving—it's dark and it's raining, but I'm driving any-way. I'm on the highway and the road is almost completely empty. There's just me in my car and a bunch of trucks. We've all got to get somewhere.

I told my parents I was going out and that I needed to borrow the car. I didn't tell them what I was going to do. It's not like they need to know, really. Maybe I should have told them, but I didn't want to talk about it, I just wanted to go.

It's raining hard now. I was going to listen to some rock music, but the rain is coming down so hard that I'm not re-ally in the mood. I found one of Mom's CDs in the glove compartment—it's the music from *Fantasia*, that Disney movie with all the classical music. I slide in the CD.

I skip forward a couple of tracks until I find the one I'm looking for. It works, just like I thought it might. The music and the windshield wipers are perfectly in sync with each other—so that every time the wipers move, the music does something too.

How long have I been driving? It's been a long time already. Two hours? The road is almost completely empty.

It's 1:11. Make a wish.

I almost feel like my brother is riding here in the car with me. I almost feel like if I look over—that he'll be sitting there in the passenger's seat, just kind of smiling and relaxing.

I don't want to look over at him, though, because what if he isn't really there? Then it will just ruin everything. I'm just going to drive like he's there.

I'm just driving in the middle of the night in the rain with my brother. That's all.

I say, "Hey, Bro. What's up?"

He doesn't say anything, of course, but I feel like he would say something if he could. I don't know what to say. I don't know if I should ask him about that night, or if I should just talk to him.

I say, "So, did I tell you about Katya? She's amazing. She really is. I don't know—I get that feeling when I'm with her. Every time I'm with her—I get butterflies in my heart. She's just so . . ."

I'm not sure this is what he wants to hear about, so I stop talking and wait for some sort of sign from him. Even if he can't say anything—at least there might be a way to communicate from where he is.

I say, "Do you want me to talk about Katya?"

There's nothing.

"Do you want me to talk about Dan and Amy and that whole mess?"

Still nothing.

"Mom and Dad—and how weird they are?"

Nothing at all.

I say, "I bet you're pretty mad at me, huh? I bet you're pretty mad because I've never been to your grave, huh?"

He doesn't say anything. I guess that means he is mad.

"What? It's not like you acted so great all the time toward me. It's not like you were always the nicest brother in the world to me, okay? You could have been nicer. You could have been a better older brother to me, okay? It's not like I did anything to you, besides being born, and I can't really do anything about that now, you know?"

I shut up and wait for him to say something. I know I was being a little mean, but I just wanted to see if I could get him to talk to me—to say something out loud. Something I can actually hear with my ears. I listen to the wind and the wipers and the music and the rain, but I don't hear anything else. I don't hear his voice.

I push the pedal down and the car speeds up. The white lines are just a blur now. There's no one else on the road.

I've got this question that I've been wanting to ask him. I don't want to scare him away. I want to ask him if he meant to do it. I say, "Did you mean to? Did you mean to do it?"

There's no answer, but I feel like he's still here. I feel like he's sitting right next to me in the passenger's seat, but I'm too afraid to look over—or try to touch him—because I'm afraid that he's going to go away and never come back.

Maybe he can't talk from where he is. Maybe he's just here to listen and not talk and just be here so he knows what I'm thinking.

Don't do it.

"I wasn't. I wasn't going to."

Don't do it.

"I don't know what the fuck you're talking about. I wasn't going to do anything."

Don't do it.

"Seriously. I wasn't going to do anything. I'm just driving. I'm not like you—you know—I'm not an asshole like you. I wasn't going to drive myself into a ditch at seventy miles an hour."

I start crying all of a sudden, because I just realized that I was sort of thinking about doing that. I was sort of thinking about doing what he did.

I'm the same age now as he was, and I don't want to be older than him. I don't want to be fucking older than my older brother.

"Do you know how that feels? Do you know how it feels to be older than your older brother? You were supposed to be here. You were supposed to be my older brother and you fucking went and messed that up. For what? Why? Why did it have to be that way?

"You're such a fucking asshole. You've always been a fucking asshole—you know that? I've always hated you. I've always hated you with everything I ever had. And now you're here telling me not to do it? Not to do what you did? Well, fuck you. I'll do what I want."

I'll fucking do what I want. I'll fucking do what I want, and you can't stop me.

"When you were driving did you know what you were doing? Did you know when you were driving and you didn't have your headlights on and your seat belt on—did you know you were going to die?"

No answer.

"Were you trying to die? Were you trying to destroy yourself?"

Maybe it doesn't even matter if he meant to do it. I mean, what does it matter now if he meant to do it or not? He did it. It doesn't really matter if he was trying to.

"I don't know why, but I get so angry about it. I just get so angry when I think about it. It didn't have to happen. I just get so angry.

"I hate that I get so angry. It's like there's all this anger in my blood and it's pumping through me all the time, and there's no way I can get the anger out of me. I don't know how to get it out of me."

I'm crying. I just hate everything so much

Let it go.

"What? Let it go? Are you kidding? Everyone says that. What does that mean? Let it go? Do they teach you to say stuff like that at the Ghost Academy? I can't let it go. It's real. It's in me. I can't let it go. It's my blood. I can't let my blood go."

Let it go.

"Let what go? What can I let go? I can't let you go. You're my brother. I can't let you go. I don't want to. I miss you too much."

Let it go.

"What? What am I supposed to let go?"

I know what I'm supposed to let go. I don't know how to do that, though.

"How do I do that? How do I let it go? I can't just do that, just because you're talking to me from beyond the grave. It's not like I have some magical power now."

I'm quiet for a while. I can't tell if he's still here.

"Are you still here? I hope you're still here."

I'm quiet again, for a long time.

It doesn't really matter if he's here or not. I can pretend like he is. I say, "Do you want to listen to some music?"

I take out *Fantasia* and slide in another CD from my mom's collection.

It's the blind Italian guy that she loves. I don't know what he's singing about, but I love the melody. It goes up and down and up again, and then way up into these notes I'll never be able to sing, but I wish I could.

My brother and I are driving around together listening to music, and that's all that matters.

The sun is coming up over the horizon and I'm here at the graveyard. How long have I been asleep? The sky is turning from black to gray, and then peach around the edges. I look over at the passenger seat. He's not here.

I remember I was here before, a long time ago, when I was little. Mom took us out here and showed us where she and Dad were going to be buried.

Yeah, she took us out here and showed us the spot. It already had a gravestone with their names and their birthdays on it. I remember thinking that was the saddest thing in the world. I unhook my seat belt and take the sign out of the backseat—the one from his bedroom door at our old house.

I think I remember where it is. It's near a big tree—because Sean and I played on the tree. We climbed it and were running around it and laughing and Mom yelled at us, because we were having too much fun in the graveyard.

I remember that exactly. I remember climbing it and sitting on that low limb, and looking down at all the gravestones stretching out across the hills. I don't remember what I was thinking, but I remember how it looked from up there.

I wonder what I was thinking back then.

Here it is. This is where he's buried. Right next to where my parents will be.

I sit down on the cold, wet grass and lean my brother's sign against his gravestone.

Maybe I'll never understand. Maybe I'll never understand.

I feel so tired. I lie down on my back and look up at the limbs of the old oak tree swaying in the breeze. I look at the sunrise filling up the world with light and the way the clouds are moving across the sky.

The ground beneath me is cold and wet, but it's not too

cold. It feels like there might be some warmth coming from somewhere in the center of the earth. The clouds are making me dizzy. I grab two fists full of grass and hold on to the earth, like it's a roller coaster and I'm not strapped in.

I hold on like the earth is spinning a thousand miles per hour—doing everything it can to throw me off. I hold on tight.

I can feel the earth spinning beneath me and the wind blowing above me. I can feel everything.

I can feel everything.

# ACKNOWLEDGMENTS

Nancy Siscoe, my editor at Knopf, was supportive, insightful, and open throughout the process.

Lisa Bankoff, my agent, gave me the initial push to begin this book and also came up with the title.

Thanks also to:

Judith Haut

Tina Dubois Wexler

Isabel Warren-Lynch

Eight Cousins Bookstore in Falmouth, Massachusetts

The Runyon, Parseghian, and Egloff families

And especially Lillie, Walker, and Hope, for making me laugh.

Brent Runyon is the author of the highly acclaimed memoir *The Burn Journals*. He is a regular contributor to public radio, including *This American Life*. This is his first novel.

Brent Runyon lives on Cape Cod, Massachusetts.

| DATE | | | |
|---|---|---|---|
| | | | |
| | | | |
| | | | |
| | | | |
| | | | |
| | | | |
| | | | |
| | | | |
| | | | |
| | | | |
| | | | |